Brad took a few steps over to the light switch. The thief gasped when he flipped it on.

But Brad was ready. He turned the young robber around so they could face each other.

"Oh." Brad still had the boy in his grip. Rather, he had *her* in his grip, he corrected himself.

"You're a girl." Brad could see she was more like a woman, but he was only starting to sort things out.

The woman glared at him. She had wispy blond hair that settled in soft curls around her face. And her face—she looked solemn and scared at the same time. The only muscles that moved were her eyelids. She kept blinking.

"You dropped my glasses," she finally said.

Brad looked back and saw where her glasses had fallen on the floor. He also saw a brown paper bag sitting on one of the café's tables. Through a tear in it, he saw money....

Books by Janet Tronstad

Love Inspired

*An Angel for Dry Creek #81
*A Gentleman for Dry Creek #110
*A Bride for Dry Creek #138
*A Rich Man for Dry Creek #176
*A Hero for Dry Creek #228
*A Baby for Dry Creek #240
*A Dry Creek Christmas #276

*Dry Creek

JANET TRONSTAD

grew up on a small farm in central Montana. One
of her favorite things to do was to visit her grandfather's bookshelves, where he had a large collection
of Zane Grey novels. She's always loved a good story.

Today, Janet lives in Pasadena, California, where she
works in the research department of a medical orga-
nization. In addition to writing novels, she researches
and writes nonfiction magazine articles.

A DRY CREEK CHRISTMAS

JANET TRONSTAD

Steeple
Hill®

Published by Steeple Hill Books™

STEEPLE HILL BOOKS

Steeple
Hill®

ISBN 0-373-87286-0

A DRY CREEK CHRISTMAS

www.SteepleHill.com

Printed in U.S.A.

...for every one that exalteth himself
shall be abased; and he that humbleth
himself shall be exalted.

—*Luke* 18:14

In memory of my dear friend
Judy Eslick

Chapter One

Millie Corwin squinted and pushed her eye-glasses back into place. The night was full of snow clouds and there were no stars to help her see along this long stretch of Highway 94. Millie was looking for the sign that marked the side road leading into Dry Creek, Montana. She could barely see with the snow flurries.

What had she been thinking? When she had told the chaplain at the prison that she would honor Forrest's request, she hadn't thought about the fact that Christmas was in the middle of winter and Dry Creek was in the middle of Montana so she would, of course, be in the middle of snow.

She hated snow. Not that it made much difference. Snow or no snow, she had to be here.

Millie saw a sign and peered down the dark

road that led into Dry Creek. Only one set of car tracks disturbed the snow that was falling. Hopefully that meant most people were home and in bed at this time of night. She planned to arrive in Dry Creek, do what she had to do, and then leave without anyone seeing her.

Millie turned the wheel of her car and inched her way closer to the little town.

She wished, and not for the first time, that Forrest had made a different final request of her while he was dying.

She met Forrest three years ago. He'd come into Ruby's, the coffee shop where she worked near the Seattle waterfront, and sat down at one of her tables. Millie must have taken Forrest's order a dozen times before he looked her in the eyes and smiled. There was something sweet about Forrest. He seemed as quiet and nondescript as she felt inside. He was restful compared with all of the tall, boisterous, loud men she'd learned to ignore at Ruby's.

It wasn't until he had been arrested, however, that she knew the whole truth about Forrest. He'd been a criminal since he was a boy and had, over the years, gotten deeper and deeper into crime until he'd eventually become a hit man. His last contract had been for someone in Dry Creek.

When Millie got over the shock of what Forrest was, she decided he still needed a friend. She had visited him while he was in prison, especially this past year when he'd been diagnosed with cancer. The odd thing was the sicker he got the more cheerful he became. He told her he'd found God in prison.

Millie was glad enough that Forrest had found religion if it made him happy. She smiled politely and nodded when he explained what a miracle it was that God could love a man like him.

Personally, Millie thought it would be a miracle if God loved anyone, but that it had more to do with God than the people He was supposed to love. However, since Forrest was sick, she supposed it was good if Forrest thought God loved him and so she nodded pleasantly.

But when Forrest added that God loved her as well, she stopped nodding.

Of course, she kept smiling. Millie didn't want to offend either Forrest or God.

Then Forrest added that he was going to pray for her so she would know God's love, too. Millie could no longer keep smiling; she could barely keep quiet. She'd always kept a low profile with God and she figured that was the smart thing to do.

If God was anything like the other domineering males she'd seen—and there was no reason to think otherwise—then He looked out for His own interests first. If He noticed a person like her at all, it would only be to ask her to fetch Him a glass of water or another piece of toast or something else to make Him more comfortable.

Millie had grown up in a foster home where she was the one assigned to do chores. Usually, the chores consisted of cooking, doing laundry and taking care of the five boys in the home.

Millie didn't know if it was because she was easier to order around than the boys or if her foster mother really believed males were privileged, but—whatever the reason—she soon realized she was doing all of the work for everyone in the house and, instead of being grateful, the boys only became more demanding.

By the time Millie left that home, she'd had enough of dealing with loud, demanding males.

And those boys were mere mortals. She figured God would be even more demanding. No, it was best if God didn't even know her name. She didn't want anyone mentioning her to Him. She had no desire to be God's waitress.

Still, Millie wasn't good at telling people what to do or not to do, and she certainly couldn't tell a dying friend to stop praying. So she changed the subject with Forrest and asked what kind of pudding he had had for lunch. She would just have to hope Forrest came to his senses on his own.

He didn't. Every letter he wrote after that said he was praying for her.

When Forrest died, the chaplain at the prison forwarded a final letter Forrest had asked him to mail.

In the letter, Forrest said he had tried to right some of the wrongs in his life. He hadn't done anything about Dry Creek, however, and he asked Millie to go to the place and try to restore the little town's innocence.

"I fear I've made them distrust strangers and I regret it," he wrote and then added, "Please go there, without telling them who sent you, and do something to restore their faith in strangers. And when you go, go at Christmas."

Millie winced when she read that line in the letter.

Even though Forrest had gone to Dry Creek at Christmas himself, Millie knew it was more than that that made him suggest the holiday. Forrest knew Christmas was a lonely time for her.

Not that she didn't like Christmas. It was just that she always felt like she was on the outside looking in when it came to the holidays. She'd made Forrest tell her several times about the little town with the Christmas pageant and the decorations. It all sounded like a picture on one of those nostalgic calendars.

In the foster home where Millie grew up, they had never done much to celebrate Christmas. Her foster mother always said she was too busy for that kind of thing. Millie had tried to make a fake Christmas tree one year out of metal clothes hangers and tin foil, but the boys had laughed at it and knocked it down.

Millie had never had a Christmas like the one Forrest witnessed in Dry Creek and now, it appeared, he wanted her to have one.

Even though the thought of spending Christmas in Dry Creek held a kind of fatal attraction for Millie, she would never have agreed to Forrest's request if he were alive and she could tell him face-to-face why his idea wouldn't work.

For one thing, Forrest was asking her to make the little town trust strangers again, and she wasn't the kind of person who could do something that would make a whole town change its mind about anything. Forrest knew that.

Even more important, Millie suspected that if the people in Dry Creek knew who had sent her they wouldn't trust her even if she did manage to sound persuasive. After all, Forrest had tried to kill a woman in their town two years ago. The people certainly wouldn't welcome a friend of Forrest's, let alone want to celebrate Christmas with her.

But Millie couldn't tell Forrest any of those

things when she got the letter, because—well, he was dead. So she did the next best thing. She called the chaplain who had mailed the letter and tried to explain why she wasn't the person to fulfill Forrest's last request. The chaplain listened and then told her Forrest had said she might call and that Forrest wanted her to know his request was important or he wouldn't have asked her to do it.

All of which was why Millie was here in the dark. She couldn't let Forrest down.

Of course, she couldn't do exactly what he wanted, either. Therefore, she made her own plan. She decided she would do what she could to restore Dry Creek's trust in strangers and she would do it at Christmas, but she would do it without actually talking to a single person. In fact, she'd do it without even seeing another person's face.

Forrest would have to be content with that.

Hopefully, she'd be able to do what she needed to do tonight, Millie told herself as she saw a few house lights ahead of her. She had gone down the road that led into Dry Creek. It was Saturday, December 22. If she left her presents in the café tonight, the people of Dry Creek would discover them on Monday, Christmas Eve Day.

By Christmas, the people of Dry Creek should all be talking about the kindness of the stranger who'd come to town in the middle of the night to bring them a wonderful surprise and who then left without even waiting to be thanked.

Maybe they'd call her the Christmas Stranger. Millie rolled her tongue over that phrase. Christmas Stranger. She rather liked the sound of that, she decided.

Brad Parker shoved his Stetson further down on his head and squinted as he tried to read his watch in the dark. Snow was falling outside and the heat from his old diesel engine barely kept the ice from forming on the windshield of his pickup. It was a sad night in Dry Creek, Montana when a thirty-four-year-old man ended his Saturday evening hiding out in his pickup without even a woman beside him to make it look like he had a reason for being there.

The worst part was, he'd already been parked behind the closed café for the past half hour, well off the road so no one could see him, and wondering when it would be safe to go back to the bunkhouse at the Elkton Ranch.

The last time he'd gotten back to the bunkhouse before dawn on a Saturday night was because of a tooth that was so infected Dr. Norris had insisted on opening the clinic to fix it even though it was Sunday—and everyone in the whole county knew

Dr. Norris never missed a Sunday church service if he could help it.

Brad had been in enough pain at the time that he'd said yes when the good doctor asked him to come to church some Sunday morning. And, Brad told himself, he meant to do just that—someday. No one would be able to say Brad Parker didn't keep his word, even if they could say he was a fool to make a promise like that in the first place when he didn't own a tie and would rather have the root canal all over again than actually go to church.

Brad ran his tongue around his teeth. They all felt fine to him. He did an internal check for other pain and found none. He appeared to be in fine health. Which was a pity, in a way, because the guys would understand him making a short evening of it if he had reason to suspect he was dying or something.

If he wasn't dying, though, they were sure to guess the truth, and that was why Brad was sitting here in the cold. It was bad enough that he knew he always got depressed around Christmas. He didn't want to have to hear about it from the other guys in the bunkhouse, as well.

He'd left the poker party early because he was heading out to another game on the other side of town. He got halfway to the game and decided he didn't want to play anymore. All he wanted was to go home. Since he was already on the road, he just kept driving until he pulled into Dry Creek.

That's when Brad realized he couldn't show up at the bunkhouse yet. If Charlie hadn't stopped going to Billings on Saturday nights, no one would even be in the bunkhouse to hear him slip in early. But Charlie fancied himself the grandfather of "his boys," and he was sure to make a big deal about Brad and Christmas.

Brad shook his head. He never should have told the guys that his parents had been killed in a car accident just before Christmas when he was small. It had been five years ago that he'd mentioned it, and every year he still caught one or two of them watching him with a certain look in their eyes just before Christmas. He didn't know why they made such a big deal about it.

It wasn't a crime to get depressed at Christmas anyway. Brad made it through the other fifty-one weeks of the year just fine. If he wanted to feel sorry for himself one week out of the year, the rest of the world should just let him.

Still, as long as he was going to bed early tonight, he might as well get up early tomorrow morning. Maybe, since his week was already shot because of Christmas, he should just keep his promise to Dr. Norris and show up in church.

Yeah, Brad thought to himself grimly as he

tried to make himself comfortable on the old seat of his pickup, he'd just get all of the bad stuff out of the way and start the new year fresh. No point in wasting a good weekend next year by going to church.

That's what he'd do. Get rid of Christmas and church in one fell swoop. But first he'd give Charlie another half hour to go to bed just in case the old man might surprise Brad and actually be asleep when he got home.

It was sure going to be some Christmas, Brad said to himself as he leaned back against the seat of his pickup and closed his eyes. Yeah, it was going to be some Christmas.

Chapter Two

Millie held her breath as the shadows of Dry Creek came into view. The little town was just as she had pictured it when Forrest told her about it. The clouds had parted and the moon was shining even though a few flakes of snow were still falling. There was one street lamp, and it gave off enough light that the flakes looked like glitter floating over the darkened town. A lone pair of tire tracks had packed down a thin path of snow on the road into town, but elsewhere snow sat soft and fluffy alongside the dozen or so buildings.

Millie could see the church with its steeple. The house next to the church had lights in the second floor windows and filmy white curtains. That must be the parsonage where the woman whom Forrest had been sent to kill lived. At the time, the woman had just been passing through Dry Creek when two little boys decided she must be an angel, and therefore just what they needed for the town's Christmas pageant.

Forrest always shook his head when he told Millie about the little boys who thought they'd found their own personal angel. Forrest had never known that kind of innocence in his own life. Of course, he hadn't been sent to kill the woman because the boys thought she was an angel. The woman had witnessed a crime, and that made some big guys nervous enough to want her out of the way.

Forrest was particularly glad he hadn't succeeded in that job.

The woman, Glory Beckett, was now married to Matthew Curtis, the man who was pastor at the church. The pastor also worked at the hardware store down the street, and Millie wished she could see that building more clearly. Millie's favorite memory of Forrest's Dry Creek stories was the part about the old men who sat around the woodstove in that building. If she were coming into town like a regular person, she would like to sit with those old men some morning and listen to them argue about cattle prices. It all sounded so peaceful. She truly wished—

Millie shook her head. She couldn't afford to

dwell on those kind of wishes. A life around a cozy wood stove in Dry Creek wasn't meant for someone like her. She had her tables at Ruby's. They might be filled with scruffy men who wanted more coffee, but that was what she had for the time being.

Millie dimmed her lights when she pulled close to the café. No one was around, but she didn't want her lights to shine into the windows of any of the houses farther down the road. She didn't pull in too close, because the snow wasn't packed down that far off the road and she didn't want to get stuck. She checked the mirror behind her as she turned off her lights. No one was coming.

Millie opened her car's door. Forrest had told her stories about the café, and so she knew the spare key was sitting under a certain rock on the porch. With any luck, she would be in the café and have her surprises delivered in less than ten minutes.

Brad wasn't sure what woke him up. It might have been the lights on the car that was driving into Dry Creek. Not that the lights themselves would have woken him up. It was when the driver dimmed the lights that something stirred his sleeping brain. When he heard the thud of a car door quietly shutting, he opened his eyes. Even then half of his brain was thinking that Linda was coming in early to open up and maybe he could get a cup of coffee.

He discarded that theory as soon as he thought it. Linda had closed the café for Christmas week so that she could go visit that boyfriend of hers in Los Angeles. Linda had said the town could use the café if anyone wanted to cook a Christmas Eve dinner like she had in the past, but so far no one had agreed to do the cooking. In any event, Linda wasn't even in the state of Montana.

Brad slid open his pickup door and woke up completely. The cold air pushing into the pickup was enough to get a man's attention. He wished he didn't have to go and investigate, but he saw little choice. Everyone knew Linda was gone, and if someone had mischief in mind, now was the time they would do it.

The snow softened Brad's footsteps as he walked along the side of the café. He looked in the corner of the window and saw a figure moving around inside. Whoever it was had thought to bring a flashlight, and the beam of the light was flickering around inside. The flashlight sealed the argument for Brad. No one who had any business being in there would bother with a flashlight when the light switch was right next to the door.

It must be some kid, Brad thought to himself.

He could see the boy's shadow and judged him to be around eleven or twelve. Brad figured a boy that young would be more nuisance than trouble. Brad looked over at the car parked in front of the café. He didn't recognize it, but it was a kid's car all right—a beat-up old thing the color of crusty mustard. It looked like it was held together with rubber bands and bubble gum—but it was still a car. Which meant the boy was probably at least sixteen.

With any luck, Brad could deliver the boy back to his parents and that would be the end of it.

Millie's fingers were so cold she had a hard time keeping the flashlight steady. She had set the bag of flannel Santa socks at her feet and the other bag, the one with the hundred-dollar bills, on the table in front of her.

It was the perfect thing to do with the money Forrest had given her before he left for Dry Creek two years ago. Millie had tried to give the seventy-five hundred dollar bills to the police, but they didn't want them because they couldn't prove they were connected to a crime. She didn't want them because she couldn't prove they *weren't* connected to a crime. She had been poor all her life, but she'd never knowingly profited from the misery of others.

Millie had fretted about what to do with those bills until she'd realized they were the solution to her problem in Dry Creek. She'd give a bill to each person in Dry Creek along with a note saying the money was from a stranger. That would make them all trust strangers more, wouldn't it? A hundred dollars would do that to most people in Millie's opinion. It sure would have caused a stir with those boys in her old foster family.

Besides, she'd be able to get rid of the money and fulfill Forrest's request at the same time. It was brilliant. And the best part of all was, she wouldn't have to actually open her mouth and talk to anyone.

Millie supposed she should have pre-stuffed the socks and written her notes, but she had decided she would do that in the café. She wanted to think about how excited each person would be when they opened their socks and saw the money.

It had not been easy, but Millie had remembered the names of most of the people who lived in Dry Creek. Forrest had sprinkled his stories with a surprising number of names and, fortunately, they had stayed in her head. She'd written names on most of the socks. In her opinion, a present wasn't really a present unless it had a person's name on it.

Some of the names might be misspelled, but

she was sure each stocking would find its owner. She even had a few labeled "Anyone," for those she might have missed. Most nights last month, after she finished at the coffee shop, she'd pick up the glue gun and personalize the Christmas socks. Before the glue dried, she sprinkled glitter on the writing.

She was proud of the socks. The money might be from Forrest, but the socks were from her.

Millie didn't know what made her think something was wrong. Maybe it was the fact that the air inside the café was suddenly a couple of degrees colder. Or maybe it was the darkness inside had grown just a shade deeper, like someone was blocking the moonlight that had been coming through the open door behind her. Whatever it was, she didn't have enough time to turn around before she felt the arms close around her.

Woosh. Millie felt her breath leave her as panic rose in her throat.

"What the—?" Brad revised his opinion of the juvenile delinquent he was apprehending. The boy might be small, but he wasn't puny. He had stomped on Brad's foot with all his might. The kid was wearing some kind of wool coat that made grabbing him difficult, but Brad had roped calves for the last twenty years and knew a thing or two about handling uncooperative creatures.

Brad grabbed the boy around the middle and hoisted him up in the air where his feet could do less damage. The boy gasped in outrage, but Brad didn't let that stop him.

"If you want me to put you down, you have to stop kicking," Brad finally said as he shifted his arms so that the kid was hanging on Brad's hip like a bag of grain. Brad had his arm hooked around his captive's stomach, and the boy's head was facing toward the café door. He wore enough wool to clothe a small army, and it bunched up around his middle. Brad was having a hard time keeping the boy from wiggling out of his arm so he could walk back to the light switch.

The boy must be deaf, because he sure wasn't doing what Brad had politely suggested. Which was what Brad would expect, considering the whole night had gone from bad to worse. Well, Brad decided, he'd had enough.

He took his other hand and pushed the wool coat up high enough so he could get a firm grip on the boy's stomach. The boy's shirt had come untucked in the struggle, and Brad figured his hand was firmly anchored around the boy's stomach.

"That's better," Brad said. The boy had gone still in his arm.

Brad took a couple of steps over to the light

switch even though something was beginning to make him think he'd got a few things wrong. The boy must be even younger than Brad had figured.

His stomach was softer than anything Brad imagined you'd find on a boy of fifteen who lived around these parts. Maybe that was the kid's problem. No one had taught him to ride horses or wrestle calves. Brad doubted the boy had even done any summer farm work. That belly had never been scratched by lifting a hay bale or sliding under a broken-down tractor.

The boy gasped again when Brad flipped the light switch, but Brad was ready for him. This time he tipped the kid upright so they could face each other.

"Oh." Brad still had the boy in his grip, or rather—he corrected himself—he still had her—*her*—in his grip.

"You're a girl!" Brad could see she was more like a woman, but he was only starting to sort things out, and "girl" would do for now. He never should have left those poker games tonight.

The girl-woman just glared at him. She had green eyes and wispy blond hair that settled in soft curls around her face. And her face—she looked solemn and scared all at the same time. The only muscles that moved on her face were her eyelids. She kept blinking.

"You dropped my glasses," she finally said.

Brad looked back and he saw where her glasses had fallen to the floor. He also saw a brown paper bag with a long tear in it on top of one of the tables. Through the tear he saw money.

Brad whistled. "I guess I don't need to ask what you're doing here."

The woman went even stiffer in his arms.

"I'm not one to judge people," Brad continued as he carried her over to the brown paper bag. He began to wonder if the woman had been getting enough to eat. She sure didn't weigh much. He could carry her around on his hip like this for hours without tiring. "I figure you're poor enough that stealing some money from a cash drawer is tempting, but you'd be much better off getting a job."

The woman relaxed some. "I have a job."

"Now, there's no need to lie to me," Brad continued patiently. "No one's blaming you for needing help. But in this town we ask for help, we don't steal from each other."

"I'm not stealing."

For such a little bit of a woman, she sure was stubborn. Brad looked at the bag more closely and frowned. Why had Linda kept that kind of money in the café? Even though break-ins were rare around here, there was no point in tempting folks.

"What's your name anyway?"

"You don't know me. I'm a stranger."

Something about the way the woman said that irked Brad. "I wasn't planning to sit down and socialize or anything—I just asked your name."

"Oh. My name's Millie."

"Millie what?"

"Just Millie."

Brad sat down in the chair next to the table. As he folded all six foot four of himself onto the chair, he shifted Millie so she sat on his knee.

Brad almost sighed. No wonder he had thought she was a kid. Even with her sitting on his lap, he still didn't meet her eye to eye. Which was a pity, because he'd been wondering if her eyes weren't more blue than green, and he'd been hoping to have another look. Of course, it wasn't because he was personally interested. It was just so he could answer the questions if he had to describe her for a police report. Looking down, he saw the top of her head. "How short are you anyway?"

That statement at least made Millie look up at him. Her face was no longer pale and scared. It was more pink and angry now. Of course, that was probably just because he'd been carrying her sideways.

"I'm just under five feet *tall*, not *short*," Millie said. "And I don't see what business it is of yours anyway."

Brad grinned. He'd always liked green eyes that threw spit darts at him. "Lady, everything about you is my business. At least until I can get the deputy sheriff to come pick you up."

That seemed to take Millie's attention away from him. She twisted around on his lap and looked at the door.

"Don't even think about making a run for it," Brad said. Until he said that, he had half a mind to give her a few dollars out of his own pocket and send her on her way. But he figured he should at least wait until she said she was sorry and promised to stop stealing from people.

"I don't run away," Millie announced.

Brad believed her. She sat as still as a stone on his lap, as if she was resigned to the worst. He didn't want to scare her. "Well, it's not like they'll probably lock you up or anything—you didn't even make a getaway."

Brad reached down and picked up Millie's glasses off of the floor, then gave them to her.

Millie took the glasses from him and settled them on her nose.

Brad frowned. Those glasses not only hid the golden tones in Millie's green eyes, they hid her face, as well. Without them, she was pretty in a quiet sort of a way. Her face was pale with freckles scattered across it. With her wispy blond hair and those solemn green eyes, she looked like pictures he'd seen of young girls living on the sunbleached prairie a hundred years ago.

She didn't look like his ideal woman, of course. Her hair might be blond, but it didn't have any of the brazen look he preferred. He liked women with red lipstick and sexy laughs who knew how to flirt.

But still, for a quiet kind of a woman, she was pretty enough. Until she put those glasses on. The glasses made her look like a rabbit.

Of course, how the woman looked was not his problem. Brad stood up and wrapped Millie under his arm again. "Sorry I don't have any rope to tie you up with. So we'll just have to make do until I get the sheriff on the phone."

Brad sat down again once he reached the phone at the back of the café. He settled Millie back on his lap. This time it seemed more like she belonged there. Like he was getting used to her. "You don't really need those glasses, do you?"

"That's none of—"

"—my business," Brad finished for her. Well, she was right. She was too serious for the likes of him anyway. He needed a woman who liked a good time and would leave it at that. A woman like the one sitting on his lap would turn her green eyes on him and expect him to make a commitment to her. He didn't need any of that. Especially not when he was depressed anyway. He reached for the phone and dialed a number. The phone rang and rang. No one answered.

Brad sighed. It was time someone dragged Sheriff Carl Wall into the twenty-first century and got him a cell phone. What were law-abiding citizens supposed to do when they apprehended a thief in the middle of the night?

Brad looked back over at the bag of money on the table. The bag was small, more of a lunch bag than anything. Still, it was stuffed full. If she'd only been stealing twenty bucks to make it to the next town, he'd probably let her go.

But seeing that bag of money gave him pause. The side of the bag was split and he could see the bills. He wasn't close enough to see the denominations, but there were probably a few hundred dollars there. He wasn't doing anyone any favors if he let a thief like that loose in the night.

"I guess I'll just have to take you in," he said finally. The Elkton bunkhouse wasn't the fanciest place around, but it was built solid and all of the locks worked. He could just lock her in his room for the night, and get the sheriff to come out in the morning.

In the meantime, Brad would throw a tablecloth over that bag of money and lock the café door. It should be safe enough until morning when he and Sheriff Wall could come back and investigate. As he recalled, the sheriff was particular about the scene of the crime, and Brad wanted to be able to tell him that he hadn't touched anything.

For the first time that evening, Brad had a happy thought. He might not need to go to church tomorrow morning after all, not when he had to clean up after a crime. Even God and Dr. Norris had to understand that keeping the law was important.

And, Brad decided, because he had fully intended to go to church, that should count as keeping his promise even if he didn't actually get there. He told himself it wasn't his fault someone had been stealing from the café.

Chapter Three

"Get in," Brad said as he held the door of his pickup open. The passenger door had a tendency to stick, and he'd had to put Millie down so he could open it. He'd kept one arm hooked around her stomach while he'd swung the door open with his other hand. "Get in."

"I never ride with strangers," Millie said as she braced herself.

Brad sighed. He could feel the woman tense up. He never knew a thief could be so particular about the company she kept. "Don't worry. No one's a stranger for long in Dry Creek—"

Well, that made her relax, Brad thought.

"Really? So you're not worried about strangers around here?" she asked as she turned around to face him. "You trust them?"

The woman sounded downright cheerful. Brad wondered why for a moment before he remembered. "We're not so trusting that we don't lock our doors, of course."

Brad lifted the woman up into his pickup and settled her on the seat. He knew he was lying a little, but he figured it was allowed under the circumstances. Some people did lock their doors when they went away for a trip—if they could find their keys, of course.

Brad figured he should drive his point home just so she knew she wasn't in some nostalgic Rockwell painting where everyone was easy pickings for any thief who might come driving by. "We've had our share of crime here. Why, we had a hit man come to town two years ago at Christmas. He tried to kill the pastor's wife."

"Oh." The woman was looking straight ahead as if there was something to see out the windshield of his pickup.

"Of course, we took care of him. Had him arrested and sent to prison." Brad congratulated himself as he shut the door on his pickup. That should let her know that the people of Dry Creek knew how to handle bad guys.

Brad walked around to the driver's side and got in.

"I'm sure he must have been sorry," Millie said.

"Who?" Brad put the key in the ignition.

"The man who tried to kill your pastor's wife. I'm sure he was sorry."

The woman's voice sounded a little hurt. Brad looked over at her. That's just what he needed—a sensitive thief. Ah, well. "You don't need to worry. The people of Dry Creek are big on forgiveness once you say you're sorry. If you just explain that you tried to take the money because you were hungry—"

"I wasn't hungry." Millie lifted her chin and continued to stare straight ahead.

Brad gave up. "Fine. Have it your way."

"I wouldn't steal even if I *was* hungry," Millie added quietly.

"Fine." Brad looked in the rearview mirror as he put his foot on the gas and eased the truck forward. He really shouldn't feel sorry for a woman that determined to be unreasonable. "But if you were hungry, say real hungry, that might explain why you had broken into the café in the middle of the night."

There, Brad told himself, he'd given the woman an excuse for being at the scene of the crime. She could say the money was just sitting on the table and she'd only been looking for a piece of bread. He wasn't sure she was smart enough to use the story, but he'd done what he could for her.

Brad turned his pickup onto the road going through Dry Creek. The town sure was quiet at midnight.

After a few minutes of silence the woman said, "I'm not a thief."

Brad figured it was going to be a long night and an even longer morning with the sheriff. He was beginning to think maybe he wouldn't be getting such a good deal by skipping out on church to re-visit the scene of the crime. What a night. He'd never imagined the day would come in the life of Brad Parker when church sounded like the better of two possibilities.

Millie's hands were cold. Ordinarily, she would put them in the pockets of her coat and they would be warm enough. But the man beside her made her nervous, and she wanted to keep her hands free. She didn't know exactly why, but it just seemed like a good idea. She'd never really liked big men, and this one had to be at least six feet tall. She could hardly see his face, not with the darkness and that Stetson he wore. Mostly, she could just see his chin. He needed a shave, but outside of that, his chin looked all right.

"I would think the jail would be back that way." Millie was trying to remember the map she'd studied before starting the drive from Seattle. The bigger towns were all west of Dry Creek. Going east, there weren't any towns of any size until you got to Minot, North Dakota. Leave it to a big man like that to have no sense of direction. Maybe he couldn't see very well with that hat on. If that was the case, she wouldn't criticize. She knew what it was like when a person couldn't see too well.

"I'm not going to the jail. I'm going home to the ranch."

"What?" Millie forgot all about being under-standing. She knew she shouldn't have gotten into the man's pickup. That was a basic rule of survival. Never get into a car with a strange man. "You have to stop and let me out. Now!"

The man looked at her. "I told you I was hold-ing you until I could get the sheriff."

Millie tried not to panic. The man was big, but he didn't look malicious. Still, what did she know? The only part of him that she'd gotten a good look at was his chin. "Usually, suspects are taken to a jail to be held for the sheriff."

"We don't have a jail in Dry Creek."

Of course, Millie thought, she knew that. "There's one in Miles City."

The man grunted. "You'd freeze to death in there this time of year."

"I have a coat." Millie put her hands in her pockets. She did have a good warm coat, and she was glad she'd brought it with her. "I'd really prefer the jail."

The man just kept driving. "I'm not driving back that direction tonight. The sheriff can take you there tomorrow if he wants. He's the one that has to okay turning the heat on anyway."

"They don't heat it?"

The man shrugged. "Budget cutbacks. They only heat it when they have someone locked up, so the sheriff tries to keep it clear this time of year."

Millie looked out the window. The night was black. It was even too cloudy to see any stars. She didn't see lights ahead that might have signaled a ranch house, either. Not that she was anxious to get to this man's ranch. "Is your wife home?"

Millie told herself to breathe. The man must be a local rancher. That meant he had to have a wife. If there was a woman around, she'd be all right. She trusted women.

The man grunted. "I'm single."

"Oh."

"Not single in the sense that I'm looking for a wife." The man reached up and crunched his hat farther down on his head. "Of course, I enjoy a date just like the next man. I'm all in favor of dating. You know, casual dating."

"Oh." Millie was trying to count the fence posts outside. How was she going to find her way back to Dry Creek when he stopped this pickup? She really wished the man had a wife. "Do you have a sister?"

"Why do you want to know about a sister?" The man's voice sounded confused. "Are you into double-dating or something? If you are, I could set up a date with one of the other guys—Randy is seeing someone pretty regular."

"Will she be there?" Millie felt her hands tense up.

"Where?"

"At your ranch."

"My ranch? Oh, ah, yeah. My ranch. I think so."

Millie relaxed. "Good."

Brad told himself he hadn't been this stupid since he was sixteen. He'd just lied to a woman to impress her. Why had he allowed her to think he owned a ranch? Hadn't she seen his pickup? It was an old diesel one. Did he look like he owned a ranch? He should have corrected her and said he worked on a ranch. Worked, not owned. Of course, he dreamed of having his own ranch, and he hoped to make that dream come true before long, but still—

And, to make it worse, the woman was a thief. It stood to reason she would only date a man with property. Of course, it wasn't like she was a bad criminal. Maybe he should tell her he was close to owning his own ranch. His ranch wouldn't be as big and fancy as the Elkton Ranch, but it would do.

Brad shook his head. Was he nuts? The last thing he needed was to fantasize about dating a woman who was a criminal.

He usually didn't fall into the trap of lying about what he had in life. Of course, he usually didn't need to—women wanted to date him because he was fun to be with. There were lots of women who would like to date him—women, by the way, who didn't have a rap sheet.

Brad shook his head again. He didn't know what was wrong with him. He shouldn't even be having this conversation with himself. Maybe he was running a fever or something.

He looked at the woman out of the corner of his eye. She sat so close to the other door, Brad could have put two other women between them. Women, he might add, who would want to sit next to him. Millie, if that was her real name, sure wasn't the friendly type.

Besides, she had that little frown. He doubted she would recognize a good time if it came up and bit her on the backside. He shouldn't even care what she thought about him.

Brad turned the wheel of his pickup. The mailbox for the Elkton Ranch stood at the gravel road that led back to the ranch house. Fortunately, the boss was off spending Christmas with his wife's family in Seattle, so no one was home in the big house. The bunkhouse was just past the ranch house.

"I live here," Brad said as he eased the truck to a stop in front of the bunkhouse. Anyone with any sense would figure out from that that he didn't own any part of this ranch.

Brad expected some question about why he lived in the small house instead of the big house, but Millie didn't seem to notice.

"Someone's home inside," Millie said. The relief in her voice made her sound happier than if they had stopped at the big house.

Brad looked at the windows and, sure enough, Charlie stood in the window looking out to see who had driven up to the bunkhouse at midnight. It wasn't until Brad saw Charlie that he realized his plan had a small problem. The bunkhouse didn't have many rules. Actually, there were only two. No wet socks by the woodstove, because no one wanted to burn the place down. And no women allowed past the main living room of the bunkhouse.

Sometimes the rule on the socks was bent. But the one about women? Never.

Charlie would insist Brad turn around and go find Sheriff Wall and deliver the suspect to him. He wouldn't care that it was twenty degrees below zero outside and Brad didn't even know where the sheriff was right now, or that the suspect in question was unfriendly and uncooperative and looked at Brad, when she had those glasses of hers on, like he was the one who had committed a crime.

Brad decided he had had enough for one day.

"Here, you might want to wear my hat," Brad turned around and set his hat square on the woman's head. The woman's glasses were the only thing that kept the hat from falling halfway down her face. "And there's no need for the glasses."

"What?"

Brad plucked the glasses off the woman's nose and hooked the top button on her black wool coat. There, she looked like a juvenile delinquent again. "Just give me a minute of quiet and I'll have you safe inside."

"Safe inside from what?" The woman's voice was rising in panic.

"Ah." Brad thought. "Spiders. The man inside keeps pet spiders."

Brad congratulated himself. All women were

afraid of spiders. But just in case. "He might have some snakes, too."

Brad could feel her stiffen up, and he felt a little bad. He pulled her across the seat to his side. "You don't need to worry, though. I'm going to carry you through to a safe place. You just need to be quiet for a little bit."

"Why?"

"Ah, the spiders go crazy when they hear any noise." Brad opened the door. The wind almost froze his ears now that he didn't have his hat.

Brad stepped out of the pickup and picked up Millie again. It didn't seem right to carry her like a bag of grain now that he knew she was a woman, but he didn't want to make Charlie any more suspicious than he'd naturally be. The truth was, those glasses of Millie's had reminded Brad that Charlie couldn't see so well at night anymore, and Brad figured there was a good chance he could slip Millie into his room without Charlie even seeing them. And he could do it, too, if he used the side door to the bunkhouse.

The door squeaked, and Brad tried to be as quiet as he could. The rooms for the ranch hands were all lined up in a row, and each had a door going off of this long hallway. At the end of the hallway was the main room where Charlie was standing by the window.

Brad held his breath. His room was only two doors down from the side door, and it would take only a little luck to reach it before Charlie figured out that he wasn't coming in the main door.

Brad put his hand on the doorknob leading into his room at the same time that he heard Charlie cough. Brad pushed the door open anyway and put Millie inside. "Stay there a minute."

Brad only waited long enough to be sure Millie was standing upright before he stepped out of the room and closed the door.

"That you, Brad? What's that you have?" Charlie asked as he peered down the long hallway.

Brad put on his best smile. "Nothing."

"Nothing?" The old man frowned.

Brad kept his smile going. "Well, Christmas is coming, you know."

"That's right." The old man relaxed and smiled as he walked down the hall toward Brad. "I forgot it's the time of year when a person shouldn't be too nosy."

"That's right. All those Christmas presents." Brad figured by now Charlie would be expecting more than the new pair of leather gloves Brad had tucked away in his drawer for the occasion. Brad figured he'd need to get Charlie a shovel or something big. Maybe a ladder would do.

"I'm glad to see you're in the Christmas spirit," the old man said slowly.

"It's a joy to give." Brad kept smiling. He wondered when lockjaw set in on a man's mouth. He figured it'd be coming any minute now.

"That's good to hear." Charlie was talking the same, but Brad noticed the old man wasn't looking at him anymore. Instead, he was looking over Brad's shoulder.

Brad turned around. Millie stood in the doorway of his room, and she wasn't wearing his hat or her glasses. She was wearing the coat buttoned up to her neck, which, with her blond curls and timid face, made her look like she was about twelve.

"I see we have company," the old man said gently.

"I thought you were going to stay in the room," Brad said.

"I'm not afraid of spiders," Millie said to no one in particular. Her face went white when she said it. "Unless they're black widows, and then anyone would be afraid."

Millie couldn't see much without her glasses. Mostly it just looked like a long tunnel with a white light at the end of it and several large rocks along the way. The closest large rock was the man Brad.

"If you have spiders, you really should make them stay out in the barn," Millie suggested. She'd taken off the hat he put on her head and looked for her glasses. "You forgot to leave me my glasses."

"Oh."

Millie didn't know why he needed to sound so annoyed. She hadn't made any fuss about the spiders. "I would imagine they'll have spiders in the jail."

"No, they won't. Too cold," Brad said as he held out her glasses.

Millie could see the arm outstretched, and she reached for the open palm. Ah, there were her glasses.

She blinked when she put them back on. Usually, she didn't blink so much. At first, she thought it was because of the light in the hallway. But that didn't make sense. Even though she couldn't see, her eyes had already adjusted to the brightness.

No, what was startling her eyes was the man. She hadn't had a good look at him until now. My goodness, he was handsome. Not that she was interested herself. The closest thing to a boyfriend she'd had in the last five years was Forrest, and he'd turned out to be a hit man. She didn't exactly have reliable sense when it came to men. But still, she'd have to remember what the man looked like so she could tell the other waitresses at Ruby's. They'd enjoy a story about a good-looking rancher who lived in a house full of spiders.

She took another good look at him so she'd remember. Brad's hair was dark as coal, she decided, and he kept it just long enough to curl a little at the ends. The hair alone made him look like a movie star. But it didn't stop there. He had the blue eyes of the Irish. No wonder his chin was strong. The Irish always had strong chins. They also generally talked a lot, and that was what the man was doing right now.

Brad had stepped closer to the old man and was whispering something to him. The inside of the room was made out of oak logs. There were beige curtains on the window and long leather couches around the room. The old man nodded several times while Brad spoke.

Then both men looked up. Millie heard the noise, too. Even with all of the snow outside, it sounded like a dozen pickups had screeched to a stop out in front of the bunkhouse.

Brad didn't bother to leave the shadows of the hallway. He wondered what had made the other guys rush home from Billings. He looked at the clock on the opposite wall. It was only twelve-thirty. "There must have been a fight. There'll be a broken bone or two."

The door opened and eight other ranch hands stomped into the bunkhouse.

"Okay, who's hurt?" Charlie demanded as he stepped into the main room from the hallway.

All eight of the men who had entered the bunkhouse stopped. "We're worried about Brad."

Brad stepped from the hall into the main room. "Why? I'm right here."

"Oh." The men flashed each other guilty looks and then stared at the floor.

Finally, Howard, one of the older men, cleared his throat and rubbed the beard on his chin. "We thought we'd check on you, that's all. Heard you hadn't made it over to the other game."

"Since when is it a crime to go to bed early on a Saturday night?" Brad was getting tired of apologizing for not spending his night gambling. Just because he didn't want to sit down with a bunch of smelly men and bet his week's salary against theirs, it didn't mean anything was wrong.

"It's just not like you," another of the men, Jeff, mumbled. Jeff was the only one who had taken his hat off when he came in the bunkhouse, and Brad could still see the snow melting on the man's shoulders.

"Whoa," Randy, the youngest ranch hand, said and then he whistled. "We take that back—it *is* like you. Going to bed early when you have company is an altogether different thing."

It took Brad a full ten seconds to realize what Randy was saying—or rather what he was seeing.

Brad turned around, but he already knew what he would see. Millie had left the hallway and was standing behind him. She was holding the neckline on her coat tight around her throat, and it made her look nervous and young. At least she had her glasses on so she didn't look as pretty as Brad knew she could.

"It's not what you think," Brad started.

"You don't need to say another word," Randy said as grinned and backed up toward the door.

"Yes, he does," one of the other hands, William, spoke up. William had been an accountant before he became a ranch hand, and with his thinning blond hair and long face, he still looked like he was always trying to balance the books. William had known Brad for the past ten years. He was looking at Brad now like he'd never really known him, though. "Isn't she too young?"

"Of course she's too young," Brad snapped back.

"I'm twenty-three," Millie spoke up.

Brad groaned. How could the woman be twenty-three and be so dumb? "She's young for her age."

William nodded, no longer upset. "Still, it's the age that counts. Sorry we bothered you."

"You didn't bother me. Nothing's going on."

Brad could see the speculation in Randy's eyes. Randy was only twenty-two or so himself, and he looked like he was realizing Millie was more his age than Brad's.

Randy swallowed and spoke. "Well, if nothing's going on with the two of you, then maybe you wouldn't mind if I—"

Brad felt his arms tighten. It had been a while since he'd taken down any of the other guys with his fists, but he could still do it. "She's not in the market. Besides, you already have a girlfriend."

Charlie cleared his throat. "Now, there'll be none of that." He looked at Brad. "That's the reason why we have the rule—no women allowed."

"She's not here because she's a woman," Brad said. "She's here because she's a thief."

Brad expected his statement to bring some dignity to the situation. Instead, William looked at him like Brad was the one at fault.

"You don't need to lie. We're prepared to make some exceptions for you on account of—" William swallowed and stared at the floor "—on account of the time of year and all. If she eases the pain some, maybe we could let her stay with you for the night."

"What?" Brad was dumbfounded. Sometimes a man broke the bunkhouse rules, but never ever was anyone given *permission* to break them. How pathetic did they think he was?

"William's right," Charlie mumbled. "She could even stay with you through Christmas, since the boss isn't here. He'll never know. You've got your own bath and everything, so the two of you will be snug in your room. She'll make you happy."

Randy and the others just stared at the floor.

Brad snorted. "You're all hopeless. She doesn't make me happy. I caught her breaking into the café."

"Really?" William asked. He looked at Millie and smiled. "You're sure she wasn't just hungry? She's awfully small to be a thief."

"I'm not a thief," Millie said.

Brad looked over his shoulder. Millie stood in the hallway in that long wool coat of hers looking like a refugee. "Then what were you doing in the café with all that money?"

"I can't say."

Brad looked at the other men. "See?"

"Does anybody recognize her?" Charlie asked. He'd taken a step closer to Millie and was studying her. "Between all of you, I figure you know every woman over the age of sixteen in the whole county."

"Never seen her before," William said.

"I'd remember her if I had," Randy added.

"I'm a stranger," Millie said.

"A stranger who happens to be a thief," Brad added.

"Maybe," Charlie said thoughtfully. "She doesn't look like any thief I've ever seen, though."

"Well, we'll find out in the morning when I can get hold of the sheriff."

"The sheriff's not in his office tomorrow," William said. "It's Sunday—he'll be in church."

"Well, then," Brad said grimly, "that's where I'll need to go to talk to him."

There was silence in the room.

Finally Randy spoke. "You're going to church?"

Brad nodded. People went to church all the time around Dry Creek. What was the big deal?

There was more silence.

"Inside the building?" William finally asked. "Not just volunteering to shovel the steps like you sometimes do when it snows?"

Brad nodded. "Of course, inside the building—"

Randy whistled. "This'll be something to see."

"There's nothing to see. I'm going to just take Millie there to the sheriff and give her a chance to confess—"

"I didn't know they still did confessions in church," Randy said.

"I don't have anything to confess," Millie said. "Well, at least not about being a thief."

"Wow," Randy said. "This'll be something to see."

Brad was annoyed. "There's no reason to get all excited. There'll be nothing to see or hear in church tomorrow. I'm just going to tell the sheriff about the scene of the crime and—"

"You mean there's a crime scene?"

Brad shook his head. It was hopeless. "Anyone want to stay out here and chew the fat? Millie needs to go to bed and get her sleep, but I'll be sleeping on the couch out here and I'm happy to have some company for an hour or so."

"No, thanks." Randy grinned. "I think I'll be getting up early in the morning."

"Me, too," William added. "I haven't been to church in a while."

"You've *never* been to church," Brad said as he sat down on a folding chair. "You're as much of a heathen as I am."

"I was baptized as a baby," William protested as he turned to walk toward the hall. "That makes me a member."

Brad shook his head. "No, it doesn't."

"I think you need to pay dues to be a member," Randy added as he turned to the hallway, too.

"Just go to bed," Brad said.

Charlie nodded. "We all need our sleep."

Brad didn't know if it was sleep he needed. Maybe an aspirin would do him more good. He had a feeling he wasn't going to sleep at all tonight, and it wouldn't be because of the lumps in the sofa.

Chapter Four

Millie had been to church once when she was a child. Her foster mother had taken her to an Easter service because the child welfare representative was going to come the next day and there was always a question on the form the man filled out about church or other religious activity.

They had gone to an old church that had big stained-glass windows that showed pictures of Jesus in many different poses. Millie had been in awe. She liked the picture best of Jesus kneeling down beside a child. The child had been wearing a blue robe, and Millie had on a blue dress that day. She looked at the picture and pretended it was her that Jesus was smiling down at and talking to in such a friendly way.

When she left the church, Millie told her foster

mother about pretending that she was in the picture with Jesus. Her foster mother said she was silly. She said those pictures of Jesus were from thousands of years ago and had nothing to do with today.

Millie still remembered the disappointment she felt. It was the first time she'd realized Jesus lived such a long time ago. Somehow she had the feeling he was supposed to still be alive today.

That was the last time Millie had been inside a church.

She was surprised that the church in Dry Creek didn't have any stained-glass windows. Of course, she remembered looking at the church last night in the dark and she hadn't seen any, but churches had always seemed mysterious places to her, and she expected to step into the church in Dry Creek and see something dramatic like a stained-glass window anyway.

Instead, the church was humble. The glass was frosted because of the cold outside, but not decorated in any other way.

There was a strip of brown carpet going down the middle of the church between the rows of wooden pews, but the flooring on both sides of the carpet was the kind of beige linoleum that she had seen frequently in coffee shops. The only problem with that kind of linoleum was that there was a special trick to getting off the black scuff marks. Millie looked down at the floor. Everything was scrubbed clean, but the black marks were still there. She could tell someone how to fix that.

Not that she was here to talk about the floor, Millie reminded herself. She was glad Brad didn't seem like he was in any hurry to actually go inside the church, either. They both just stood in the doorway.

There were quite a few people in the church already, but they weren't sitting down yet.

"Do I look all right?" Brad whispered down at her.

Millie looked up. She was getting used to Brad's face. Well, sort of.

Maybe it was because she'd spent the night on his pillow and grown accustomed to the warm scent of him that lingered in his room even as he slept in the other room on the sofa. When you've been in someone's bed like that, she thought, handsome didn't seem to matter so much.

Besides, he didn't seem to care that he was handsome, so that helped some more. He was mostly worried about the tie he had around his neck. He'd had to borrow it from Charlie this morning, and Charlie only had two ties and said he needed one for himself. Charlie kept the black one, the one he called his funeral tie.

Brad had had to settle for a red tie with elves on it that Charlie had won in some bingo game at the senior center in Billings last year.

Millie nodded. The elf tie did go, in a way, with the green shirt Brad had borrowed from William.

"I feel stupid wearing dancing elves around my neck," Brad said.

Millie wasn't used to men admitting they felt stupid. "They look a little like drunken mushrooms."

"Really?" Brad seemed cheered by the idea.

Millie nodded. "At least I have my coat to wear."

Millie had bought the black wool coat years ago because it covered everything. She could have her waitress uniform on and no one would know. She didn't always like people to know she was a waitress when she rode the bus to work. Too many men felt they could flirt with any woman who was a waitress. Of course, the men were usually harmless. But still, she didn't want to be bothered.

Brad was frowning down at her. Millie wondered if maybe the coat wasn't too protective. She didn't want men to scowl at her, either.

"I could hold your glasses for you," Brad said finally.

What was his problem with her glasses? That

was the second time this morning that he had suggested she not wear them. "My glasses are fine."

Brad nodded. "I thought they might fog up so you couldn't see. You might not know that. Glasses do that in the cold."

"I'm fine."

Brad nodded again, "Well, we might as well go in then."

There was a double door that led into the Dry Creek church, but only one half of it was open this morning.

Millie felt Brad take her elbow at the same time that they took a step into the church.

"Oh." Millie wished she had given her glasses to Brad. At least then she wouldn't see all the people who had turned around to look at them. There were tall people, old people, short people, and children. They all seemed like they were talking—until she and Brad walked into the church.

"Well, welcome!" A ripple of excitement went around the people standing in the church.

"Why, Brad Parker!" An older man stepped forward and held out his hand. The man was wearing a tweed jacket, and he smelled of old-fashioned aftershave.

Brad shook the man's hand. "Good morning, Dr. Norris."

"I'm glad you came." The older man wasn't

content with a handshake. He slapped Brad on the shoulder, as well.

"I told you I'd come," Brad said.

Millie was glad Brad didn't move. She was also glad he was so big. She could almost hide behind him as long as he stood just where he was. Maybe no one would notice she was there.

"And welcome to you as well, young lady," the doctor said as he stopped looking at Brad and looked over at Millie. "We're glad you've come to worship with us."

"Oh." Millie gave a tight little smile. "I don't know if we'll be staying for—"

"Of course you have to stay for the service." An older woman stepped forward and beamed at Millie. "We're singing Christmas carols, and the Curtis twins are going to practice their donkey song—you know, the donkey who carried Mary to the Inn?"

"You mean the twins—Josh and Joey?"

"Why, yes," the woman said. The woman had her gray hair twisted into a mass of curls on the top of her head, and she was wearing a green gingham dress with a red bell pin. Millie knew who the older woman was before she held out her hand.

"My name's Mrs. Hargrove," the woman said.

Millie nodded and took the woman's hand. She

never thought she'd get to meet Mrs. Hargrove. Mrs. Hargrove had written to Forrest several times while he was in jail. That's why Forrest knew so much about Dry Creek. And to think, Millie would hear the twins sing. Oh, she hoped Brad didn't want to meet with the sheriff before she could do that. "My name's Millie."

"How did you know about the twins?" Brad asked quietly.

Millie looked up at him and saw the suspicion in his eyes. She'd have to be more careful. "I thought you mentioned them last night."

"Me?"

"Well, maybe it was William—he brought me an extra blanket in case I got cold and stayed to talk for a little bit. Did you know he used to do the books for a restaurant in Seattle?"

"William what? I thought you were going straight to bed. That's what everyone was going to do."

"Well, I couldn't go to sleep if I was cold, could I?"

Someone started to play the organ, and Millie was relieved to see everyone starting to sit down.

Brad was still scowling. But at least he'd stopped looking down at her, Millie thought.

"I don't see the sheriff here," Brad said.

"He'll be here any minute," the older man, Dr.

Norris, said, as he gestured to the pews. "You're welcome to sit anywhere."

"I think we should sit at the back," Brad said. "In case Sheriff Wall gets here soon."

The doctor nodded.

Millie was glad that the sheriff wasn't there quite yet. She and Brad walked to the last pew and sat down. Brad seemed to relax. He even loosened his tie.

Now that Millie was getting a good look around, she noticed that someone had decorated the small church for Christmas. There was a short, stubby tree with tinfoil stars on it by the organ. Some of the stars were crooked, and they all looked like children had made them. Mixed in with the stars were some red lights that twinkled. Several poinsettia plants stood in front of the speaker's stand.

Some years at Ruby's they had poinsettia plants on the counter at Christmas. Once or twice the manager had given Millie one of the plants to take home after her shift ended on Christmas Day. They were hardy flowers and lasted almost till Easter.

"No one's wearing a tie, except for Pastor Curtis," Brad whispered in her ear. "I thought everyone wore a tie to church."

"This is sort of an informal church, I think," Millie whispered back.

Millie heard some sounds behind her and turned around. There stood all of the men from the Elkton Ranch bunkhouse, looking shy and out-of-place in the doorway.

"Welcome," the pastor said quietly from the front of the church. "Please take a seat anywhere."

The men filed into the back pew on the other side of the church, and the service started.

"I don't sing much," Brad whispered as everyone around them stood with a songbook in their hands.

"Me, neither," Millie said as she stood up. She figured it didn't matter if you sang or not as long as you stood up at the right time and were respectful.

Singing wasn't as hard as Millie had thought. Some of the songs were Christmas carols that she knew from the radio that played at Ruby's, and she joined in the singing of those—quietly, of course.

The church service reminded Millie of a roller coaster she'd ridden once. She was scared at every turn of the corner, but she found she enjoyed it if she sat back and didn't try to fight the experience. Being in church was kind of like that.

There was a light behind the wooden cross in the center of the church, and Millie decided she could stare at that. She wasn't sure she was supposed to be listening to the sermon since she was just here to wait for the sheriff, so she didn't want to keep her eyes on the preacher. Of course, she couldn't help but hear the sermon. It was something about grace.

Millie wasn't quite sure what it all meant. The pastor had said grace was when you got something for free, but the only time Millie had heard of grace was at Ruby's when sometimes a customer would pray before they ate. One of the other waitresses said the people were saying grace. Millie wondered now if the people had been hoping they would get their dinners for free and not have to pay. She was surprised Ruby hadn't put a stop to people saying grace if that was the case.

No one got a free meal at Ruby's unless they happened to be really down on their luck. Then Millie sometimes paid for their meal out of her tips for the evening. Millie wondered if grace was something like that. When she gave out a free meal because another person was hungry and couldn't buy the meal for themselves. She'd have to ask the pastor if that's what grace was.

Of course, she'd have to wait until Brad turned her over to the sheriff and the sheriff turned her loose. She didn't suppose the pastor would want to talk to a woman who was in the process of being arrested.

Millie's favorite part of the whole church service was when the Curtis twins put on their donkey faces and sang a song about taking Mary to the Inn. They walked up and down in front of the church like they were on a long journey. Once one of the twins brayed like a donkey and pretended to fly. That had to be Josh.

Millie hadn't thought about how difficult it must have been for Forrest to learn so much about the people of Dry Creek in the few days he was in the little town. Even with Mrs. Hargrove's letters, there was a lot he learned himself. He said he'd talked to people in the café and even stopped at a few houses to ask directions here or there and had stayed to chat.

"People will tell you anything if you get them talking," Forrest said to her once when she asked how he did it. "Everyone likes to talk."

Millie wished Forrest were here. He'd know what to do about the mess she was in. Of course, if he were here, he'd probably want her to continue on with her mission. She hoped Brad was right and that the people of Dry Creek did trust strangers. If they didn't, she sure didn't know how she'd get them to trust strangers now.

When the service was over, the pastor stood at the back door to shake hands. The men from the Elkton Ranch were the first ones in line. In fact,

Millie suspected a few of them had tried to beat the pastor to the door so they could go through it before he even got there. But Charlie made them get in line.

Brad and Millie were right behind them.

"I'm glad you could join us this morning," Pastor Curtis said to Randy as he shook the younger man's hand.

Randy blushed and ran his finger around his necktie to loosen it. "We mostly came in to see the crime scene."

"What?" That was from Mrs. Hargrove. She was coming up to greet the men, too. "I know our singing isn't too good, but I'd hardly say it's a crime scene."

"No, ma'am." Randy turned even redder. "I mean the crime scene at the café."

A ripple of whispering went through the whole church until everything got silent.

"A crime! Has anyone seen a stranger?"

A gasp came from another corner. "Has anybody been shot this time?"

Millie looked around her. Forrest was right. He had taken away this little town's trust in strangers. She could see it in the faces around her. They were scared.

"It's nothing like that," Brad said gruffly. "Just a little bit of—well, maybe something was stolen."

"We have a thief?"

"I'm not a thief," Millie denied automatically. She wished she hadn't said anything when everyone turned to look at her.

"Well, of course you're not," Mrs. Hargrove agreed. "Anyone can see you're a nice young woman." The older woman smiled at Millie. "I was so pleased you were able to convince Brad to come to church with you."

Millie blushed. "Brad came to see the sheriff."

"Well, still—" Mrs. Hargrove kept smiling. "I can't believe you were stealing anything." The older woman looked up at Brad. "Are you sure she didn't just stop at the café thinking it was open and she could get something to eat? Maybe she was hoping to find a sandwich. Maybe she was hungry. Linda would have given her a sandwich if she had been there."

"That was a mighty green sandwich she was taking out of there. I was hoping to catch up with the sheriff so I could show him where I left everything." Brad looked around. "I thought he'd be in church this morning."

"He had something to do in Miles City," Pastor Curtis said. "But he's planning to be at our house for lunch, so he should be here any minute."

Millie looked around. She saw skepticism on a lot of faces. "I wasn't taking the money. I was trying to give it away."

Brad nodded. "Give it away? Where'd you get it from in the first place?"

"I can't tell you where."

Brad snorted. "You're going to have to think of a better story than that if you expect Sheriff Wall to go easy on you."

"I think I hear the sheriff now," the pastor said. "Maybe we should go over to the café and get this settled."

Millie looked around. The faces that had been smiling weren't smiling at her anymore. They weren't exactly frowning, but she could see the caution in everyone's eyes. "I didn't do anything wrong."

"I'm sure you didn't," Mrs. Hargrove murmured as she patted Millie on the arm.

Millie noticed Mrs. Hargrove didn't look her in the eye when she said those words, however. Mrs. Hargrove had obviously reconsidered her confidence in Millie.

It wasn't the first time since Forrest died that Millie wished she could have a few words in private with him. If Forrest could see her now, he would have to agree that she wasn't the person to make everything better with the people of Dry Creek. She was going to make it worse. Even Mrs. Hargrove didn't believe her.

"He should have sent an angel," Millie muttered. Dead people could do that, she figured. There were supposed to be lots of angels up there.

"What?" Mrs. Hargrove looked startled.

"Who's 'he'?" Brad bent down and asked. "Do you have an accomplice?"

"How many of them are there?" someone else asked.

"It's me. Just me," Millie said. She had never felt more alone in her life.

"It's best if you tell the truth." Brad frowned down at her. "I should have figured you had someone else in this with you. He probably sent you in as bait and—" Brad whistled "—I left the money right there for him."

Brad took Millie's elbow. "Let's go."

Millie had to almost run to keep up with Brad's long steps. The air outside was cold, and she hadn't had time to put the collar up on her coat. She could feel the air all the way down as she breathed it in. "You don't need to hurry."

Brad only snorted and kept walking. A dozen other people were trailing after them. "Don't know why it took me so long to figure it out—of course, a woman like you has a man around. Even Randy figured *that* out. With those eyes of yours, of course there's a man around."

"I don't—" Millie started to protest and then decided to save her breath. He wouldn't believe her anyway. They'd soon be inside the café, and he would see for himself that the money was still there and there was no man in sight.

Millie wondered how she had made such a muddle of Forrest's request. The people of Dry Creek would be even more suspicious of strangers after she left. Millie looked up at the determined set of Brad's chin and corrected herself. She should have said if she left. If she was able to.

The rancher didn't look like he'd let her leave anytime soon. She almost wished she did have some man someplace who would come get her. Although, as she looked at the rancher again, she didn't know what man she'd ever known in her life that she would put up against the one in front of her.

She looked at Brad again. Had she heard right? Did he think her eyes were pretty?

Chapter Five

Brad turned the handle on the door to the café before he remembered he had pushed the button on the other side of the handle and locked the door when he left last night.

"The key's under the rock," Mrs. Hargrove offered as she stood at the bottom of the steps. "The third rock on the porch there by your foot."

"But I have—" Millie said softly.

Brad didn't listen to Millie. Instead, he let go of her arm and bent down to turn over the rock. It was a piece of granite from the hills in the area, and snow was lodged in its crevices. It looked like Linda had hauled half of the mountain down here to place around her café. Some of the rocks outlined a dormant flower bed, but the rest of the rocks were just scattered here and there on the wide porch.

Brad decided that, when this was all over, he was going to ask the sheriff to do a public service talk on how to lock a door and keep it locked. Someone needed to pull Dry Creek into the modern age. What was the point of locking a door when a person left the key under a rock a mere four feet away? Except— "There's no key here."

"—That's because I have it," Millie said as she put her hand in the pocket of her coat and pulled out the brass key.

"You have it." Of course, she had it, Brad told himself as he took the key she offered. He hadn't asked himself last night how Millie had gotten in. "I suppose you turned over every rock on this porch hoping to find a key."

Even as Brad said that, he looked at the other rocks. They were all covered with snow. No one had moved them in the last few days. Which meant Millie hadn't turned over every rock to find the key; she'd turned over only one. "How did you know which rock it was under?"

"Someone told me."

Brad didn't know how a voice as quiet as Millie's could give him such a splitting headache. He supposed he had begun to hope that she wasn't really the thief he had first thought her to be. That she was just going inside the café to get out of the cold and maybe to fix a sandwich for herself. He was even beginning to think that Linda might have left the money there in a brown paper bag and that Millie was just counting it.

The rock took away all of those comfortable illusions. "Someone must have scouted out the town. The whole thing was planned and premeditated."

Millie frowned. It wasn't much of a frown, but Brad noticed that the tiny lines in her forehead made her nose smaller, which made her glasses slip a little bit. When she spoke, her voice sounded hurt. "I wasn't going to do anything bad. 'Premeditated' makes it sound like murder or something."

Brad heard the gasp at the bottom of the stairs. He knew the whole congregation had followed him and Millie over to the café, so he wasn't surprised that everyone was listening. The gasp came from one of the Curtis twins. It was Josh. The boys were six years old and fascinated with the usual boy things. "Did she say murder?"

"Nobody is going to murder anyone," Brad said firmly, turning around. He didn't want the rest of the people to start thinking in that direction. "This is Dry Creek. We're not like Los Angeles, where they have murders on every street corner."

"We almost had a murder here," the Kelly girl reminded him as she twisted her ponytail. She stood off to the side of the porch in an old, worn parka.

Brad wished he could remember her first name. All he knew is that she had two older sisters that he sometimes saw in the bars in Miles City. He knew *their* names, not that it did him a lot of good with this girl. He'd just have to take a guess. "Now, Susie—"

"I'm Sarah," the girl corrected him. "Remember there was that hit man that came here? So you can't say it never happens." The girl turned her eyes from Brad and stared at Millie. "Maybe she's one, too."

Josh gasped again and turned his blue eyes up to Millie, as well. "Does she have a gun?"

"Of course she doesn't have a gun," Brad said automatically before he remembered that he hadn't really checked. "At least, I don't think she does—"

Brad was remembering that coat Millie wore. She could have a cannon tucked in the corner of that thing and the wool was so heavy it wouldn't even make a bulge. But she hadn't been wearing that coat the whole time, had she? Surely, he would have noticed if she was armed. She was too skinny to hide anything without the coat. Unless, of course, it was in the pocket of the coat.

Brad wished he'd just taken Millie to the jail

last night. This was all getting out of hand. Where was the sheriff anyway? Brad ran his finger under his collar. It took him a minute to think of something to reassure the kids. "If she had a gun, she would have shot me by now."

"Some man came and tried to shoot my mom," Josh said to Millie. Josh was missing a front tooth, and he leaned toward Millie when he spoke. "That was before she was my mom."

"It happened at Christmas time, too," the Kelly girl insisted. "Right after the Christmas pageant. And we're having another pageant this year—I wonder if someone will be shot this year."

"I don't have a gun." Millie knelt down so she could look Josh in the eye. "You don't need to worry."

Brad snorted. He figured worrying was the only smart thing they *could* do, given the state of affairs. He took a side step closer to Millie and looked down at her. He really should find out if she had a gun. "I should frisk you."

"What?" Millie said as her eyes looked up to meet his.

Brad had a sudden vision of running his hands up and down Millie's coat. The problem was, the coat was so bulky he'd have to run his hands under her coat. He wasn't sure he should do that in full view of everyone. At least not with the kids around. Maybe if she wasn't wearing that coat, he could see if she was armed. "You should take your coat off."

"But it's cold."

Brad nodded. He'd tried. "We'll leave it to the sheriff. Where is he anyway?"

"I hear him," Mrs. Hargrove said. "He's using the siren."

Millie cleared her throat and turned so she faced the people waiting at the bottom of the porch. The air was cold, but most of the coats she saw were unbuttoned and unzipped. Everyone was looking at her so intently; they didn't even seem to notice the cold. Millie wasn't sure this was an ideal moment to try to explain, but sometimes a woman had to deliver her message any way she could. "Just because a man's a hit man, it doesn't mean he's a bad man."

"What?"

Millie figured the bellow behind her came from Brad. It was close enough to cause her ear damage, but she continued. She smiled at Josh and Sarah both. "Maybe the hit man was real sorry for the things he did and wished he could do something to make it all better."

Millie stopped there. She'd done her best. She hadn't gone against Forrest's wishes and said she knew him, but she'd come close. Surely, someone in the crowd would read between the lines and understand what she was trying to say. Mrs. Hargrove was puzzling something out. Surely, *she* would understand.

Millie figured she'd been understood when Mrs. Hargrove stepped up on the porch looking like she'd puzzled her way to some conclusion and was ready to speak.

"Are you a reporter?" the older woman demanded to know.

"Me?" Millie asked, aghast. "I could never be a reporter." Millie could think of a hundred reasons why she wasn't a reporter. "I don't even know how to type."

Mrs. Hargrove bent over slightly and looked at Millie's hands. "You've got a tiny ink stain on one finger. Maybe you write in longhand."

"Well, I write, but it's not the news," Millie protested. Didn't Mrs. Hargrove know that shy people never became reporters? They would have to talk to people. All kinds of people. The woman could just as well have asked if Millie was an astronaut who flew to the moon. "It's more like— well, I take orders for things."

Millie could tell by the faraway look in Mrs. Hargrove eyes that she wasn't listening anymore. She was, however, thoughtful. "Now that I think of it, I'm surprised we haven't had more reporters snooping around doing some kind of a sequel to the story they did back then—they were quite interested in our hit man and the angel. I must admit it was a good angle. And here it is Christmas again. People might be interested in seeing what had happened to the town where it all took place."

"I swear I'm not a reporter." Millie raised her hand. She'd place her hand on one of those Bibles people were holding if they wanted her to. "I don't even know any reporters."

"Well, let's hope you know a lawyer or two," a man's voice came from the back of the crowd.

Millie looked up. That must be the sheriff. He wore the uniform and—everything. She gulped. He had a gun.

Millie blinked and pulled the collar of her coat closer around her neck. "I don't know any lawyers, either."

The sheriff nodded. "I expect the county will have to get you one then. Not that they'll be happy about it. They don't even want to pay for heating the jail this time of year."

The sheriff stepped in closer and looked at Millie intently. She felt like a bug under a microscope.

"Unless, of course, you have money to pay for your own attorney," the sheriff added hopefully. "That would be good. My cousin over in Miles City works cheap. You might be able to hire him."

Millie thought of the remaining tip money she had in her purse and shook her head. "I used all my money driving here. I just have enough to get back."

"Where are you from?" the sheriff asked casually.

"Seattle."

"Lady, are you crazy?" Brad asked as he turned his back on everyone and jabbed the key into the lock on the door. "Driving all that way to rob us in Dry Creek? Let me tell you, the odds weren't great that you would find much money just lying around anywhere in town."

Brad shoved the door to the café open.

"I already told you. I didn't find the money here. I brought it with me."

Brad was tall enough that his shoulders filled out the doorway as he stood and turned on the light. "Yeah, and I'm the tooth fairy."

Millie took a deep breath. With a little bit of patience, she could explain everything to the sheriff. She could still keep Forrest's identity secret. She could just say that someone wanted to repay the people of Dry Creek, and she was the delivery person.

Millie heard Brad's low whistle before she stepped into the café, too.

"Don't touch the crime scene," the sheriff said as he stepped past Millie.

Brad had removed the tablecloth that he'd draped over the money last night.

"But look at these!" Brad had bent down and pulled one of the flannel Christmas stockings out of the sack on the floor. He had a look of horror on his face as he held it up. "I didn't get a good look at these last night."

Mrs. Hargrove and the pastor stepped ahead of Millie, too.

"Someone made them," Mrs. Hargrove said.

"I didn't have a pattern for the stockings," Millie said a little defensively. What did they expect? She'd relied on glue and hand-stitching to finish the stockings. Fortunately, she'd found several large remnants of red felt at a fabric store.

"It has Elmer's name on it," Mrs. Hargrove said, turning to tell everyone.

By now, half of the town of Dry Creek had come through the open door.

Mrs. Hargrove held another sock that Brad had pulled out of the sack. "This one says Jacob."

Millie could hear the murmur.

"I could see how a person might guess the name Jacob," someone in the back said. "But Elmer? I bet there's not fifty people left in the world with a name like Elmer."

"And here's Pastor Matthew and Glory." Mrs. Hargrove held up two more stockings.

The sheriff turned to Millie. "How do you know our names?"

Millie closed her eyes. "I was just doing a favor for a friend. He wanted to do something nice for Dry Creek, and he asked me to help him. That's all."

"We don't even have a phone directory anymore that lists everyone," Mrs. Hargrove said as she looked at all of the stockings on the table. "I'm not even sure I could sit down and write out everyone's name—not without a picture or something in front of me."

"My friend had a very good memory," Millie said. "He knew everyone's name."

"Is your friend Santa Claus?"

Millie looked down at the last question. Little Josh was looking up at her with hope in his eyes.

"I want a train," he said. "One that runs on the tracks and has a whistle. My dad says they're expensive, but I'm sure Santa Claus has one."

"My friend's not Santa Claus," Millie said softly as she knelt down to look the boy in the eyes. "But if he knew you wanted to have a train, he would have sent one to you. My friend's dead."

"Is he in heaven?"

"I—ah, well, I—" Millie didn't believe in heaven, but the little boy was looking at her with such innocence that she couldn't tell him that. And who knew? Maybe he was right. She certainly didn't know anything about it.

"My mother's in heaven," the boy said. "It's real nice there. I bet they have lots of trains. Maybe your friend could send one down from there—a super-duper flying train. Do you think they have flying trains in heaven?"

"I—ah—I wouldn't know," Millie finally managed to say.

"Me, neither," the boy agreed. "You have to die to go to heaven."

Millie nodded. "That's what I've been told."

"Looks like you've been told a lot of things," the sheriff said. His voice was not friendly like the young boy's. "Mind if I ask some questions?"

Millie rose to her feet. She supposed it was too much to ask to be left alone so she could keep talking to Josh. "Go ahead."

"First, where are you from?"

"Seattle."

The sheriff wrote something in the black notebook he'd pulled out of his shirt pocket.

"That hit man was from Seattle," said an older man who had entered the café late.

"What brings you out this way?"

"I was doing a Christmas favor for a friend."

The sheriff looked a little interested in this,

even though he didn't write anything in his note-book. "And who would that friend be?"

When Millie didn't answer, the sheriff looked over at Brad.

"Oh, no, it's not him," Millie protested. She didn't want anyone to suspect him of anything. "I don't even know him—not really. He was just doing his duty when he took me to his ranch last night—"

"His ranch?" The sheriff frowned. "You mean the Elkton place?"

"Is that your last name?" Millie turned to Brad. It was funny, she thought, that she hadn't heard his last name after all the time they had spent to-gether. Of course, the time was hardly social, so she supposed it wasn't surprising. "I saw the name on the mailbox this morning."

The sheriff snorted and turned to Brad. "Did you tell her you owned the place?"

Millie saw the red creep up Brad's neck and said the only thing she could think of. "I think maybe I'm the one who assumed it was his place."

"But I didn't correct her," Brad said.

The sheriff shrugged. "Well, I suppose that doesn't matter. I guess it stands to reason you'd try to impress a pretty girl."

Millie pulled her coat a little tighter around her. She didn't much like it when Sheriff Wall said she was pretty. "We came to church this morning to see you."

The sheriff nodded. "Sorry I wasn't there. Now, answer me this—did you plan to take this money away from the café?"

Millie relaxed. "No."

The sheriff frowned. "So you're maintaining your innocence? You're saying you weren't in here last night planning to steal this money?"

"No, I was giving the money away."

Mrs. Hargrove gasped. "Don't tell me it's charity!"

Millie looked over at the older woman. She seemed more upset than she had been all morning.

"I bet it's that church in Miles City." Mrs. Hargrove was nodding emphatically as she turned to look at the rest of the townspeople. "Remember last year they wanted to give us food baskets? I told Pastor Hanks we didn't need their pity."

"Of course, we don't need any pity," the older man at the edge of the group said. "We can take care of each other."

"It's not charity," Millie said softly. "It's a gift from someone who cares about each of you."

"Maybe it's from Doris June," the old man said as he looked over at Mrs. Hargrove. "You told me she was doing pretty good at that job of hers in

Alaska now that they gave her that big raise. Isn't she making another ten grand a year now?"

"Even if she is, my daughter knows better than to throw her money away like this."

"I wasn't throwing it away," Millie protested. "I was trying to do the right thing."

Sheriff Wall put up his hand. "No sense in anyone getting all stirred up until we find out where the money came from. Mrs. Hargrove, do you have that telephone number for Linda down in Los Angeles?"

The older woman nodded. "It's at home."

"Well, would you mind calling Linda and asking her how much money she had in the cash register when she left?"

"I'll be back in a minute." Mrs. Hargrove turned around and started toward the café door. "And while I'm there, I'm going to call that Pastor Hanks and give him a piece of my mind. Charity—we don't need charity. The people of Dry Creek are doing just fine."

She slammed the screen door on her way out.

"Now—" the sheriff looked around at everyone in the room, "—I'm going to ask everyone to step outside. Until we know otherwise, this is a crime scene in here, and I intend to keep it pure."

Millie looked around. The day was warming up, and sun streamed in through the windows.

Most people kept their coats open, so they must be comfortable in the café even though it wasn't heated. They were all standing around the tables.

Millie thought the old man who was at the side of the room, the one who had been talking earlier, might be Elmer. And the couple sitting down at a table were probably the Redferns. The woman looked pretty enough to have been a cocktail waitress in Vegas, and she was holding a baby who looked like he was a year old. Forrest hadn't met her when he was in Dry Creek, but he'd heard about her in a letter Mrs. Hargrove had sent to him.

The people started walking toward the door. Millie turned to join them.

"Not you," the sheriff said as he put his hand on Millie's arm. "You stay with me. I need to ask you some more questions."

Millie nodded. She supposed she'd have to expect questions. At least until Mrs. Hargrove was able to talk to Linda and find out that the money hadn't been left in the café when Linda went away.

"In the meantime, why don't you count that money?" The sheriff nodded toward Brad. "Give us some idea of what we're talking about here. Misdemeanor or felony."

Millie was glad that Brad wasn't leaving with

the others. She didn't feel exactly comfortable with the sheriff, not when he was asking her all of those questions. She wasn't sure that Brad believed that she wasn't a thief, but she did feel safer with him around.

Brad looked up. "They'd give her a hard time if it was a felony."

The sheriff nodded.

"I don't think she intended that much harm," Brad said as he walked over to the table that held the bills. "She probably just wanted some traveling money. That car of hers looks like it'd fall apart if someone sneezed in it. She probably needs to repair it, and I'd guess that'd take a fortune."

"There's nothing wrong with my car," Millie said before she remembered the ping in the engine. And the hiccup in the carburetor.

"That car needs to be taken out and given a decent burial," Brad muttered.

Millie frowned. She was slowly figuring out that the reason she felt safe with Brad was because he saw her as a kid instead of as a woman. Not that she wanted him to look at her like he wanted to kiss her or anything. But it was annoying to be around him and realize he was so totally immune to her charms.

Of course, she wasn't exactly swooning over him, either. Granted, he was tall and powerful.

She supposed most women would fall at his feet. Fortunately, he wasn't her kind of man at all.

She'd always thought that if she was going to be attracted to a man it would be a man who was quieter. Someone who didn't always require attention and service. Someone who would be content to blend into the background with her. A man like Brad didn't blend at all. He stood out and demanded attention.

No, she shook her head, Brad wasn't even close to her ideal man. She should be grateful he didn't notice her. And if he wanted to treat her like a kid, so much the better. She'd just treat him like a—a— Millie sighed. She couldn't treat him like anything but what he was. The most gorgeous man she'd ever seen, with or without her glasses on.

Chapter Six

"Well, how much money is there?" the sheriff asked.

Millie had sat down on one of the chairs and loosened her coat. The sun was shining in through the windows and had warmed up the café considerably. The red-and-white floor gave the place a cozy feel. There were a dozen small tables in the place. Millie wouldn't mind working in a small place like this if she ever left Ruby's.

Brad grunted in answer to the sheriff's question. He had sat down at a different table and counted the bills.

Millie didn't need to hear Brad's answer to know that there were seventy-five hundred-dollar bills in that sack. She supposed that was more than enough to be a felony. She wondered how far

she should carry Forrest's request to not let anyone in Dry Creek know she was his friend. Surely,
he wouldn't want her to actually be arrested.

"It's not as much money as it looks like," Brad
said slowly. He didn't look at either Millie or the
sheriff. "I didn't quite get it all counted, so I don't
have an exact count. But I'd guess it's under a
thousand."

Millie sat up straight at Brad's answer. "There's
more than that."

Brad wanted to put his head down and bang it
against the table. Here he was trying to keep Millie out of jail, and she was doing nothing to help
him. He clenched his teeth. "I'm sure there's not
enough here to warrant felony charges."

"Oh," Millie said.

Finally, the woman looked like she was coming to her senses. At least she didn't argue with
him again about the amount of money on the
table. What was Linda doing with all that money
anyway? Business at the café hadn't been *that*
good.

Brad wondered if Linda and that boyfriend of
hers had managed to sell the farm they had just
bought. Brad rather hoped not. He had his eye on
that place himself, and almost had enough saved
to put a good down payment on it if it came on
the market again.

"Well, it's fine with me if it's not a felony," the sheriff said. He'd picked up a few pieces of paper with tweezers and placed them in a bag. "I'd just as soon not do the extra paperwork."

Brad nodded. "Looking for fingerprints?"

Sheriff Carl Wall nodded without much enthusiasm. He was a decent sort of guy. He wouldn't be any more comfortable than Brad would be if they had to send Millie away on felony charges.

Brad looked over at Millie. The woman should sit in sunlight more often. The light filtered through her short blond hair and made her look almost angelic. She just didn't look dishonest, and that fact made Brad hesitant.

Brad had always thought he was a pretty good judge of people. A thief should look like a thief—at least when he looked in her eyes. Brad had been looking in Millie's green eyes and not seeing anything that made him think she was lying.

"Not that it'll do much good even if I do find fingerprints," Sheriff Wall continued. "This is a public place. People can have their fingerprints all over here and it's not a crime. Besides, Millie didn't actually take the money off the premises. Don't know if I'd have enough to ever get it to trial. Plus, there weren't any witnesses."

Brad nodded. "I sure didn't see anything."

Brad decided he'd done more than his share of

good deeds for the day. He'd gone to church and stayed through the sermon. He'd even sung a hymn or two. Then he'd had mercy on a poor woman who obviously needed someone to take care of her. "I guess it's sort of like grace."

Millie looked up at him and blinked.

Brad stood up and walked over to where the woman sat. "You know, the pastor in church talked about grace. That's how it is for you—not having to go to prison and all. We'll just call your sins forgiven."

Brad sat down in a chair across the table from Millie. He was pleased with himself. Maybe he should go to church more often. He seemed to have a flair for making moral points.

"I didn't ask for forgiveness," Millie protested softly, and then bit her lip. "I don't have anything to be forgiven for—at least, not with the money. The money is mine to give away."

Brad frowned. Well, maybe he wasn't so good at making those points after all. But then the woman looked tired. Not that she wavered in what she said. He had to admire the fact that she had stuck with her story. She was tenacious for such a little thing. He was kind of growing to like her. "Do you ever flirt?"

Millie looked startled.

"I was just wondering. You're always so serious." Brad had never been attracted to a serious woman until now. He supposed it must have something to do with the Christmas season. He was all out of whack around Christmas.

"Men don't respect you when you flirt with them."

Brad shrugged. "Sometimes it's just a way of being friendly."

Millie was quiet for a moment, and then she looked down at the top of the table. "That's what some of the other waitresses said. And then they told me I'd get more tips that way."

"You're a waitress?" Brad was surprised. Usually waitresses did know how to flirt. Millie's co-workers were right—they did get more tips that way. He knew he always gave a little extra to someone who had entertained him with a joke or two.

Millie looked up at him. "What's wrong with me being a waitress?"

Brad spread his hands. "Nothing. Some of my favorite people are waitresses."

It was odd, Brad thought. When Millie looked so serious, those glasses somehow suited her face. She was as solemn as a Madonna, but she looked good. Maybe it was just the sun in her hair and the defiant look in those eyes of hers.

"I can flirt," Millie lied. What was it about that

man that made her want to prove him wrong on everything? It was a good thing he didn't ask her if she could fly.

Maybe it was the arrogant way he sat there and seemed to assume someone should pay attention to him. He was the kind of man she usually didn't want sitting at one of her tables at Ruby's. Not that he'd probably be worried about that. He wouldn't starve. If he ever did get to Ruby's, the other waitresses would fight over bringing him his order.

"I just don't think it's honest to flirt with someone so they give you a bigger tip. A tip is for the service," Millie finished.

"And the smile," Brad said and paused. "I know a nice smile has cheered me up when I've been discouraged. I think that's worth something."

"Well, yes, of course. It's always good to be friendly."

Millie knew she sounded about as prim as a country schoolteacher. The truth was that she couldn't flirt with men because men, real men, scared her a little. Of course, she couldn't admit that to someone like Brad. "I flirt with short men."

Brad frowned at that. "How short?"

"Shorter than me."

"But you're not even five feet tall."

Millie nodded. "Short men need encouragement, too."

"I'm pretty short," Sheriff Wall offered. He had been quiet, and Millie had forgotten he was there, but he had obviously been listening. "Maybe a bit more'n five feet, but short enough to need encouragement."

"You're the sheriff. That's encouragement enough," Brad said.

The sheriff walked over to the table. "Maybe, but if the lady likes short men, I thought I should put my hat in the ring. She's not going to find any men around here who are shorter than me."

"She doesn't like short men."

Sheriff Wall smiled. "Just because you're six-four, there's no reason to be cross. Plenty of women like tall men. You should leave a few for the rest of us, especially if they like short men."

Millie figured the sheriff was right. Plenty of women did like men as tall as Brad. Somehow the thought wasn't as comforting as it should have been. She looked over at Brad. "I suppose you have someone special anyway."

Brad grinned. "I'm free as a bird."

Millie blinked. She couldn't believe she actually cared.

Brad heard the knock on the café door before it became a pounding. He was enjoying the pink that was covering Millie's face, though, and he didn't much want to get up and answer the door.

It was slowly occurring to Brad that Millie might have cured his Christmas blues. He hadn't had a discouraging thought since he'd met her. Of course, that might be because he'd been busy trying to figure out whether or not she was a thief.

Maybe he should do something like this every Christmas. He didn't suppose, though, that he could count on the café to provide him with a thief just before Christmas every year.

"Are you going to answer that?" Millie finally asked.

Brad looked at Sheriff Wall. "You're the public servant."

Sheriff Wall snorted. "That doesn't mean I get the door."

Still, the sheriff stood up and walked over to the door. Halfway there, he stopped and looked back at Millie. "Just remember, Brad's too tall for you."

Millie blushed a bright red.

Brad smiled. Now she looked like a Madonna with a sunburn.

Millie turned to look at the door. Maybe if she ignored Brad and his teasing, he would stop looking at her like that—like he knew something that she didn't, and it was causing him to smile like a simpleton.

"I'm not really six-four," Brad whispered to

Millie. "If I take my boots off, I'm only six-three. I'm shorter than you think."

"I don't care how tall you are."

Millie turned all of her attention to the doorway. It wasn't difficult to do, because Mrs. Hargrove was waving something at the sheriff and trying to talk.

"Let me get my breath," she finally said.

Mrs. Hargrove was standing in the doorway and taking deep breaths. She looked like she'd been running or, at least, walking fast. Her gray hair was a little disheveled and her coat was unbuttoned.

"You should have taken it easy getting back," Sheriff Wall said as he helped Mrs. Hargrove to a chair. "We're not in any rush."

"But—the money's—not Linda's," Mrs. Hargrove said as she sat down.

Millie could see the sheriff frown.

"Did you say it's not Linda's?"

Mrs. Hargrove took a deep breath. "No one left any money in the café. I talked to Linda, and she cleaned out the cash drawer to buy her plane ticket. She also said she wished she hadn't, but that's a different matter."

"So that means…" the sheriff began thoughtfully.

Everyone was silent for a moment.

"How about that church?" Brad asked. "You know, the one with the Christmas baskets."

Mrs. Hargrove shook her head. "I called Pastor Hanks. He thought I was nuts. He said they don't have that kind of money to give away in Christmas baskets, especially this year. They're giving canned green beans and some of those fried onion rings, so people can make a Christmas casserole. Then he said it had been a hard year and asked *me* for a donation. I told him I'd send him five dollars."

Everyone was silent for another moment. Millie kind of liked the silence she found in Dry Creek. There wasn't any traffic noise. There were no airplanes flying overhead. There weren't even any barking dogs, although she supposed that was only for the moment.

"So the money was hers," Brad said finally as he looked at Millie.

Mrs. Hargrove beamed. "That means she's innocent."

"Still, something's funny," the sheriff said as he scratched his head. "For one thing, she made an unlawful entry here even if it was because she was hungry or something."

Millie swallowed. She'd forgotten about using the key to get inside the café. That had seemed like the least of her worries.

"Not that that's worth locking her up over," the sheriff continued. "Not with the heating problems over at the jail and all. It costs fifty bucks a day just to keep a prisoner in jail this time of year, and the café is open to everyone."

"I'm sorry about the breaking and entering," Millie offered.

"See, she's sorry," Brad added.

Millie looked at Brad. He was looking at her like she'd just passed some sort of test and he'd guided her through it. If she wasn't mistaken, the man actually looked proud of her. Millie couldn't remember the last time anyone except Forrest had been proud of her.

The sheriff nodded. "Still, we have to do something. We can't have strangers thinking they can come into town and break into a place of business and nothing happens."

"I could pay a fine," Millie offered. Now that the money was hers again, she could use one of the hundred-dollar bills to pay the fine. She could take it from one of the extra stockings. "If it's a small fine, that is. I don't have too much extra."

"How far are you planning on driving?" Brad asked incredulously. "That money in there would take you to either coast."

"The money's not for me." Millie realized the people of Dry Creek had not suspected she was going to put the money in their stockings. Which meant that she just might pull off a Christmas surprise after all.

The sheriff shook his head. "I'm not doing some kind of fancy fine. It'd be one thing if it was a traffic fine, but I'd have to drive into Miles City just to get a form for a special-circumstance fine."

"Well, you give parking fines all the time," Brad said. "Charge her with one of those."

Sheriff Wall looked at Millie. "Might be better to just give her some community service to do."

Mrs. Hargrove brightened. "We do have a lot of work left to get ready for Christmas."

"Christmas?" Brad frowned. "I was thinking community service would involve something like picking the litter off the roads or something. I could help her with that. But Christmas—"

"No one can do litter removal with all this snow unless they have a bulldozer," Mrs. Hargrove said. "Besides, we've always done a good job of celebrating Christmas in Dry Creek." Mrs. Hargrove looked at Brad. "Just because you don't like Christmas, it doesn't mean it's not a good community-service project. Besides, it's time you got over your problems with Christmas anyway. It'll do you good."

Brad stared at her. "Who told you I have problems with Christmas?"

"Everybody knows." Mrs. Hargrove shrugged. "Why do you think we let you park behind the café last night and didn't bother you?"

"You knew I was there?"

Mrs. Hargrove looked at Brad. "Christmas can be a hard time when you have memories you would rather forget. But as far as I know, the only remedy is to make new memories."

"I don't have any memories," Brad protested, and realized it was true. And that's what bothered him most about Christmas. Other people could talk about the happy times they had shared with their families at Christmas. But he couldn't recall any. He was five when his parents were killed in the car accident, but he didn't remember any Christmases before that. Surely, he should have some memories of Christmas.

"What would I do for Christmas?" Millie asked.

Brad thought she looked a little too eager for someone facing community service. Brad turned to the sheriff. "It's not supposed to be fun, you know. She can't just decorate a Christmas tree or something."

"She could help get ready for the church service," Mrs. Hargrove said.

"I could help you get those black streaks off the floor," Millie offered.

"You know how to do that?" Mrs. Hargrove asked.

Millie nodded.

"Then you're an answer to my prayers."

"Well, I can't just let her run around free, either," the sheriff said as he looked at Mrs. Hargrove. "I don't suppose you would—"

"I'll be happy to keep an eye on her."

Brad snorted. "She'd sweet-talk her way around you in no time."

Mrs. Hargrove's eyes started to twinkle, and she nodded to Brad. "Maybe you should join us then."

"What?" The sheriff frowned. "Oh, I don't think that will be necessary. I planned to keep an eye on her myself."

Brad grinned. Mrs. Hargrove might be old, but she understood a young man's heart. It didn't always need to be the short man who got a break with the new woman in town. Brad turned to the sheriff. "Don't you have to be on duty?"

Sheriff Wall grunted. "No more than you do."

"Things are slow at the Elkton Ranch this time of year. I'm sure they can spare me for a little civic duty."

Millie was bewildered. It sounded like both of the men actually wanted to spend time with her. And they'd have to watch her mop a floor to do it. That didn't sound like any fun. "You'll get your shirt dirty standing around."

"I have some old shirts," Brad said.

"And I have some extra scrub brushes just waiting for a volunteer," Mrs. Hargrove said. "We've tried everything on those black streaks."

"I'll bring some coffee for a break when I come by in the morning," the sheriff said. "No point in anyone starting today. Besides, it's Sunday."

Brad turned to Millie. "I have some extra old shirts. You'll probably need one, too. I'll get you fixed up when we get back to the bunkhouse."

Sheriff Wall frowned. "I don't know if she should stay at the bunkhouse."

Millie agreed with the sheriff. "I don't mind the jail."

"Oh, you can't stay in the jail, dear," Mrs. Hargrove said. "It's cold this time of year. Besides, I think the bunkhouse might be just the place. Charlie will keep an eye on things."

"She can have my room. I don't mind sleeping on the couch."

"Well, it's all set then," Mrs. Hargrove said as she pointed to the money and then looked at Millie. "I guess that's all yours then. Keep it in a safe place."

"The bunkhouse is safe."

The sheriff nodded and looked at Millie. "Just

don't go spending it too fast. I plan to make a couple of inquires just in case there've been any other thefts recently in the area. I should hear back today."

"Just as long as you know by Christmas," Millie said. She would want to have the stockings ready before Christmas Day. She was glad that things seemed to be working out. She didn't mind spending a couple of days in Dry Creek.

Millie looked at Brad. He was still smiling.

"Does everybody here drink the same water?" Millie asked. Maybe there was some kind of mineral in the water around here that made people smile a lot. She'd heard about places where the population was a little below average in intelligence because of a tainted water supply. She supposed a mineral that got into the water supply could have a similar effect on emotions.

"I guess we do," Mrs. Hargrove said. "We all have our own wells, but it comes from the same water table."

Millie nodded. "I was just curious."

Brad couldn't help but see the change that came over Sheriff Wall. The sheriff had been leaning against the wall by the door, and he straightened up. The smile left his face. His eyes narrowed like he was thinking.

"What kind of stuff do you figure you need to

clean those black streaks off the floor?" he finally asked Millie.

Brad wondered why the sheriff was that interested in floor cleaners and then realized the man probably wasn't. Something else was going on here.

"I thought I'd get some baking soda," Millie said.

Mrs. Hargrove nodded. "That might work."

The sheriff was silent for a moment. "I've got baking soda at the office. I'll bring some out for you tomorrow. No point in buying any new."

"Oh, I don't mind," Millie said. "It won't take long to get some. And, if that doesn't work, I know another trick or two."

"Best to use county supplies since it is a public building."

"I wouldn't call the church a public building," Mrs. Hargrove protested. "I mean, it's open to the public, but we're independent."

"Still," the sheriff said, "I think it's best."

He turned toward the café door and motioned to Brad. "Mind if I have a word with you before we head out? You know, to explain your duties and all."

"Sure." Brad got up. He wasn't sure what was making the sheriff look older than his years, but he expected he would soon find out. He was pretty sure it was related to this floor-cleaning project.

Brad had scarcely stepped out onto the porch and closed the café door behind Sheriff Wall than the sheriff started to talk.

"I don't like it," Sheriff Wall said. "All them chemicals and cleaners—who knows what she's up to? Especially when she's asking about our water supply."

"You're not worried she's planning to do something to our water?"

"Well, not the water. It'd be hard to hit all the wells. But I didn't like the fact that she was asking," the sheriff said. "The way I figure it, that money could be payment for doing something— maybe the something just hasn't happened yet."

"Oh, I don't think—" Brad began to protest, but then he remembered. Dry Creek wasn't the same place that it had been before the hit man had come two years ago. He could no longer just assume that the only crimes in town were kids being mischievous.

Sheriff Wall nodded. "All I'm saying is that we need to keep an eye on her until we know how she came by that money."

"Maybe she saved it," Brad suggested. He didn't like to picture Millie as a criminal.

The sheriff shrugged. "Even if she saved it, what's she doing carrying it around in a brown paper bag? Most anyone I know who saves that kind of money keeps it in a bank or gets a cashier's check or something."

Brad had to admit the sheriff had a point. What would a waitress be doing with that kind of cash on her? And all in hundred-dollar bills. It wasn't her tip money, that was for sure.

"I'll keep a close eye on her," Brad said. He felt another headache coming on. The only good thing was that he figured this Christmas would be one he'd always remember.

Mrs. Hargrove thought he needed memories. Well, it looked like he was going to have them whether he wanted them or not.

He couldn't help smiling a little. He guessed he did want them, especially if the memories included a little bit of a woman with green eyes.

Chapter Seven

Millie drove her car back to the bunkhouse at the Elkton Ranch thinking the rest of the day would be spent in Brad's little room. Not that that was bad. She supposed it was better than a jail cell. The room was warm, and he had lots of books that she could read. She wouldn't mind dipping into a mystery novel or taking a nap.

Brad had driven his pickup right behind her all the way to the bunkhouse. He said it was so he'd be sure she didn't get stuck in a snowdrift, but she knew he was also making sure she didn't drive off now that she had the money.

Millie smiled to herself. All in all, it hadn't gone so badly. She hadn't been forced to tell anyone that she was in Dry Creek because of Forrest. Now if she could just avoid any other questions, she would do fine. The more she thought about it, a quiet afternoon all alone in Brad's room sounded perfect.

Millie hadn't stepped all the way into the bunkhouse before Charlie came trotting over to the door.

"There you are!" Charlie said as he held out his hand for Millie's coat. "I was hoping you'd get back soon."

Millie looked up. Charlie was looking directly at her. "Me?"

Charlie nodded. "We need a woman's advice about the Christmas tree."

"Christmas tree?" Brad asked. He had followed right behind Millie through the bunkhouse door. "Since when do we put up a Christmas tree?"

"We decided this year should be different since we have company," Charlie said as he smiled at Millie. "Mrs. Hargrove called to tell you to dress in old clothes when you go down to clean the church tomorrow."

"Oh, I will." Millie slipped out of her coat and gave it to Charlie.

"Mrs. Hargrove is the one that said you'd be staying with us through Christmas," Charlie added as he turned to walk to the corner closet.

Brad decided the world had gone crazy. Charlie had shaved off his beard, and he usually didn't do that until spring. In addition, he was carrying Millie's coat to the corner closet as if they didn't always leave their coats in a pile on the one chair. And, unless Brad missed his guess, Charlie was also wearing his church shirt, and here it was the middle of the afternoon! Granted, it was still Sunday, but Charlie usually couldn't wait to change into his working clothes whenever he came back to the bunkhouse.

Plus, Brad took a tentative sniff, he could smell cinnamon.

Brad looked around. The smell was coming from the black woodstove that stood in the corner of the bunkhouse living area. He didn't have to walk over to see the tin can sitting on the stove. "Who's cooking cinnamon?"

Charlie was back from the closet and had the decency to blush. "I saw it on TV—you put a stick of cinnamon in some water and boil it. It makes the air fresh for holiday company."

Brad needed to sit down. He walked over to a straight-back chair that was sitting next to the stove. "I thought that's what coffee was for."

"I wasn't sure Millie liked coffee," Charlie said anxiously. "I didn't see her drink any at breakfast."

"Of course she likes coffee," Brad said. He had to move a bowl of popcorn so he could sit down. "She's a waitress."

Brad held the bowl of popcorn on his lap.

"Don't eat any of that!" Charlie ordered. "That's for the tree."

Brad looked down at the popcorn. "We're really having a tree? A live tree? Not just one of those tinfoil things that they sometimes give away at the diesel fuel place in Miles City?"

Charlie nodded emphatically. "Of course we're having a real tree. We've got to have a proper Christmas tree if we have company."

Millie blinked. She had never been someone's Christmas company. Charlie said it like it was an honor. A sliver of panic streaked through her. "I've never helped with a tree before."

Brad looked up from his popcorn and frowned. "Never?"

Millie shook her head. "I think they're pretty, of course. But I usually just got myself a poinsettia plant or something like that. A tinfoil thing would be just fine with me."

"Didn't your family celebrate Christmas?" Brad asked.

Millie blushed. "My foster mother was always too tired."

Brad gave a low sympathetic growl.

"Not that I minded," Millie said quickly. "I didn't need to have Christmas."

"Well, don't you worry about a thing, we're

going to have just as much Christmas as we can right here," Charlie said. "And we're starting with a tree. How hard can it be to do a Christmas tree? That lady on television gave a few pointers. I'm sure we can figure it out."

"But there's a lot to having a tree. For one thing, you have to have decorations, and we don't have any," Brad said. "Everyone knows you need decorations."

"Well, Jeff's gone to Miles City to look for decorations," Charlie said. "All we need to do is get the stand ready for the tree, so that when he gets back we can go chop one down before it starts to snow again."

Brad frowned. "Where are you going to find pine trees this far down from the mountains?"

"We'll find something," Charlie said. "As I recall, there's a few pines on the north side of the ranch near that gully."

"But those trees are the windbreak for the north pasture," Brad protested. "The boss will have our hides if we chop them down. Besides, the cattle won't have any shelter then."

"Well, we wouldn't chop them all down. All we need is one little Christmas tree. The cows won't miss that. Then we'll get the popcorn strung and see what other decorations Jeff brings back."

Millie felt like she'd fallen down the rabbit hole and entered a whole new world. She was surprised she didn't have visions of sugarplums and reindeer dancing in her head. Actually, come to think of it, she did seem to have a little ringing in her ears. "Do you have any aspirin?"

Charlie looked over at her and thought a minute. "I think they'd be too small for decorations, but they are white, so maybe we could glue them on to something red."

"The aspirin's not for the tree," Millie said. She was beginning to feel the responsibility of being the Christmas company. No wonder so many people came to Ruby's for Christmas dinner. All they had to do then was pay for dinner. They didn't need to provide inspiration. "And— ah, speaking of the tree, I hope you're not doing anything special just because I'm here. I don't mind not having Christmas. Really. I usually don't do all the Christmas things anyway."

"Don't you worry about Christmas," the old man protested at the same time as he turned to scowl at Brad. "And don't think that we're going to let you mope around this Christmas, either. That's okay when it's just us guys here. But it's not okay when you have company."

Millie decided she really needed that aspirin. Or she would if she had to listen to Brad say one more time that she wasn't his company, wasn't his girlfriend, wasn't his date—wasn't his anything.

"You're right," Brad said simply. "I do need to cheer up and stop thinking about myself."

Millie looked at him skeptically.

Brad smiled at her slightly.

Millie looked at him and frowned a little.

Brad grinned and just kept looking at her.

"No one said where there was an aspirin," Millie finally said.

"I've got some right here." Brad handed her a small tin.

"I never take aspirin," Millie said as she snapped the tin open. Half of the eight tablets were already gone. She took out two of the remaining ones and handed it back to Brad.

"Neither do I," Brad said as he picked out two tablets for himself. "Neither do I."

Brad decided he was going to do Christmas right if it killed him—which, in this case, it just might. If he had a brain in his head, he would drive Millie back to town and let the sheriff take over guarding her. Let the county pay a few bucks to heat the jail. He'd even bring her a tinfoil tree to set in the window.

Brad no sooner thought of it than the picture of Millie spending Christmas in jail passed by his mind and he knew he couldn't do it, not even if he went in and sat in the cell with her and the little tree.

No, he had to make Christmas special for her. He had thought he was the only one who had never done any of the usual Christmas things, but it seemed like Millie might have him beat. She seemed more clueless about Christmas than he did. And he would have to be blind not to see the wistful look on her face when someone mentioned the Christmas tree.

"Can't we just tie the tree to that pole lamp or something? You know, the cast-iron one with the bear?" Millie asked as she watched him carefully select two pieces of lumber to make a Christmas tree stand. They were out in the barn and the wind was blowing in the open door. Millie was sitting on a bale of hay. Brad had the light on even though it wasn't more than three o'clock in the afternoon.

"The tree would be all crooked that way," Brad said. Ever since he'd decided to celebrate Christmas, he was determined to not take any shortcuts. Not that the lamp idea was a bad one. Charlie had won that lamp at some senior bingo party, and it would bear the weight of a tree—it just wouldn't keep it straight.

Still, it was kind of sweet of Millie to sit there with that little frown on her forehead and worry about how to save him the time and effort of building a stand. "Besides, it's not a problem. I can make a tree stand in no time."

Brad had built line shacks and corrals. He knew a little about engineering and carpentry. A tree stand wasn't even a challenge, but he wasn't in any particular hurry to finish the task and head back inside where all the other guys were sitting around stringing popcorn.

"Well, I guess if it's a small tree, it'll work," Millie said as she stood and walked over to look down at the lumber. "It will be a small tree, won't it?"

"It'll have to be. A large one will be too big for the horses to drag."

"Horses?" Millie stepped back. "Aren't we going in the pickup?"

Brad shook his head. "Too much snow this time of year. The horses are a better way to get there."

"But I've never ridden a horse."

Brad looked up at her. She looked a little scared and nervous and he decided that her look must be growing on him, because he didn't consider all of the other options that they had. "Then you'll have to ride double with me."

Brad held his breath. He wasn't at all sure that she would want to ride double with him. She might not know it, but riding a horse double was almost a date in Montana. After all her talk about short men and flirting, he'd gotten the distinct impression that she didn't want to date anyone and, if he was honest, she especially seemed not to want to date him.

"I don't know…isn't it cold?" Millie asked.

"You can wear my parka. It's down-filled and good for twenty below zero."

Brad didn't add that the lining was some kind of special silk and he'd spent a month's salary on it.

"But what about you?" Millie looked up at him, and her green eyes were full of concern.

"Don't worry about me. I'll keep warm," Brad promised. He was slowly realizing he'd like nothing better than to have Millie lean into him as they rode his horse back to the ranch. He'd ride without a shirt or a coat if he had to, just to have her trust him like he was picturing in his mind.

Millie still had that little frown on her forehead.

"I can borrow one of the spare coats," Brad added, and watched as her frown lifted. He congratulated himself that she cared about him and his comfort.

"You wouldn't be able to drive the horse if you got too cold," Millie said.

"Oh." Brad decided maybe she didn't care as

much as he'd hoped. Brad drove a nail into the lumber he had set for the tree stand. There was no need to prolong the task. He drove in another nail. "You don't need to worry. The horse knows the way back to the ranch anyway. Even if I couldn't ride him, he'd make it back to his stall."

Millie nodded.

Brad hammered the final nail into the lumber and stood up. "Here. We've got us a tree stand."

Brad opened the barn door for Millie and followed her out into the yard of the ranch. Snow covered most of the ground, although it had been pretty well stamped down from all the feet that had walked over it. The air was cold, and Brad saw Millie put her hands in the pockets of her long black coat. "I'll lend you some gloves, too."

"I can just put my hands in the pockets of your coat," Millie said.

"Not if you plan to stay on the horse."

Brad regretted his words the moment they were out of his mouth. He could tell Millie was worried, so he added, "Don't worry. I won't let you fall off."

Millie knew something was wrong the minute she and Brad stepped inside the main room of the bunkhouse. There were two long strings of popcorn garland running between the bear lamp and green recliner. There were Christmas carols playing on a small CD player. What there wasn't any sign of was peace on earth and goodwill toward men.

All of the men in the room were hunched over something on the floor by the stove, and they were clearly arguing.

"I tell you it's wrong," Charlie said as he studied what looked like a large piece of white paper. "It doesn't look like any angel I've ever seen."

Millie walked over to the men. Someone had drawn a crayon picture of an angel—at least she thought it must be an angel. "Are those wings?"

"See, she can tell those are wings," Randy said triumphantly.

"She was *asking* if they were wings," Charlie protested. "That's a big difference."

Randy looked up at Millie. "It just didn't seem right putting wings on an angel like it was some big chicken or something. I mean, what's something like an angel doing with chicken wings? I think their wings should look more like a horse's mane. You know, rows and rows of curling hair. Now, hair is nice. It's got class. It's fitting for someone who lives in heaven."

"I notice the wings are blond," Brad said from behind Millie's shoulders. "You always were partial to blondes."

"That's an angel you're talking about," Charlie said. "Show some respect."

"Well, she's not an angel if she doesn't have wings," Brad said. "She's just a good-looking woman in a white nightgown with lots of blond hair. Lots and lots of hair."

"She kind of looks like that country-western singer with the big—" William began and then looked at Millie and blushed "—with the big hats."

Charlie cleared his throat. "I hope you're not planning on putting any—hats—on the angel. We run a respectable place here."

"We're a bunkhouse," Brad protested.

Charlie lifted his chin. "As long as we have Christmas company, we're a home, and a home has certain standards."

Brad was speechless.

"Wow, that's kind of nice," Randy said. "It's good to have a home at Christmas."

Brad looked over at Millie. How was it that one woman could make their bunkhouse a home for Christmas?

Come to think of it maybe that was why he got so depressed at Christmas. Christmas was a time for families, and every year when the holiday came around it reminded him that he was alone. All he had to do was listen to a song on the radio or pass by a display in a store to know that Christmas was for families. That must be it.

Brad was almost relieved. It was all because of decorations and ads that he was depressed. Everyone had to face the advertising world at some point and realize that just because someone in an ad had something it didn't mean he had to have it.

No, he just needed perspective. He certainly didn't need to change his being single. All he had to do was get through these few days each December.

He just needed to remember that Christmas was only one day. He still had the other 364 days left to enjoy his bachelorhood. The advertising world didn't make so much of families the other 364 days.

Yeah, he had the good life. Once he got past Christmas, his life would be normal again. He'd be worrying about a poker hand instead of popcorn garlands. It would all be fine. Christmas would be here and gone soon. Maybe even quicker if he could hurry it along. "We better go see about that tree."

"I rigged up a sled for the tree," Randy said as he stood up and brushed his hands off on his jeans. "My horse can pull that easy enough."

"I figured I could bring the ax," William offered.

"But you can't just leave the Christmas drawing," Millie protested.

"Oh, yeah," Randy said as he bent down and rolled the paper up. "I'll need to finish it after we get the tree up so we can put it on top."

Brad nodded numbly. It shouldn't surprise him that they were going to have an angel who looked like a Vegas dancer sitting on top of their Christmas tree.

"I'll have some cocoa waiting for when you get back," Charlie said as they all started to look for their coats. It took a minute for everyone to realize Charlie had hung the coats up in the closet. No one ever hung up the coats.

Brad almost shook his head. He wasn't the only one who was going crazy at Christmas. Randy was drawing angels and Charlie was turning into Little Miss Homemaker.

It was going to be a miracle if they all survived this Christmas without turning into city gentlemen with manicured nails who refused to change the oil in their car. Before long, they'd all be useless.

And it was all her fault, Brad thought as he looked at Millie.

How could one woman who looked so small make such a big difference in this old bunkhouse?

Chapter Eight

Millie felt like she was in a snow globe as she rode behind Brad's saddle. The sun was setting, but there was still enough light to see the snowflakes fall. The air was so cold it felt brittle, but Millie found the steady sway of Brad's horse comforting. The landscape dipped into a long gully and then rose to small hills all around.

Millie couldn't remember the last time she'd been in a landscape with such openness. She didn't see any houses or roads or telephone poles. All she could see were stretches of white snow and the hoofprints the horses had made on their way into the gully where the pine trees stood.

Charlie was right. The cows wouldn't miss the small tree they had cut and strapped onto the sled that Randy pulled behind his horse.

They had debated which tree to cut until they saw the little tree. The branches on the tree were crooked, and William, after studying the ground around it, said they were doing the poor thing a favor by cutting it down. It was surrounded by taller trees and wasn't getting enough sunlight to grow properly.

The tree reminded Millie of that tree she'd tried to make long ago out of tinfoil and metal hangers. The tree was spindly and deformed, but somehow it tugged at her heart.

Millie turned her head around. It was getting dark, but she could still see Randy and William following behind them. She quickly turned her head back. The gap between her and Brad's back when she turned let cold air between them. Millie shivered. She was glad she had Brad's back to block the wind that came with the snow flurries.

"Sorry," Millie whispered. She suspected the borrowed coat Brad was wearing wasn't nearly as warm as the parka he had lent her, so she leaned against him as closely as she could so that at least his back would be warm.

"No problem," Brad mumbled.

All of the horses kept their heads down as they walked into the wind, and Millie knew Brad kept his head down and had his wool scarf tied around his mouth. A bandanna kept his hat tied down and his ears warm.

Millie settled into her place on Brad's back. She rested her cheek against his one shoulder and wrapped her arms more securely around his waist. She had to lift the edge of his coat in order to hold tight to his waist, and she worried that in doing so she left room for a draft of cold air. She had offered earlier to put her hands on the outside of his coat, but he had declined, saying she'd freeze her fingers.

Millie could feel the snaps on Brad's shirt, and she kept her hands clasped around the snap just above his brass belt buckle. Her hands had made a warm spot against his stomach, and they were cozy there.

Millie wondered why she felt so comfortable pressed against Brad's back this way. Well, maybe "comfortable" was the wrong word. It was more a feeling of belonging than comfort. It must be because, with her hands clasped around his stomach, they had started breathing to the same rhythm. Or maybe it was because she could be so close to him and she didn't have to worry that he was going to turn around and want to talk or anything.

Millie sighed. It wasn't easy when you were a shy woman to spend any time around an outgoing man like Brad. She'd been a waitress long enough to know men like him weren't happy with simple conversation; they wanted witty remarks and flirtatious comments. The few times Millie had gone out with men like that she'd learned she wasn't what they were looking for in a date. Those dates had been disastrous, and she wouldn't care to repeat them.

It was too bad, she thought. There was something about Brad that she was growing to like, especially now as they rode through the darkening night. If only they could ride like this forever and not have to talk.

"You can see the lights of the bunkhouse," Brad said through his muffled scarf. "We're almost home."

Millie nodded and snuggled a little closer. Brad pulled on the horse's reins and she could feel his muscles ripple down his back. She thought for a second that she would have to remember to tell the other waitresses about this ride, but then she realized she never would. This night belonged only to her. Even though she could hear the hooves of the other horses behind them stepping on the snow, it felt like she and Brad were alone outside.

"I don't mind if you take it slow getting back," Millie whispered.

She felt Brad's muscles tense. He probably thought she was crazy.

"It'll be easier on the horses," she added. She didn't want to be pushy. "They must be cold."

"They're fine," Brad said.

Millie nodded.

Brad had never been so glad to see the shape of the Elkton Ranch barn come into view. And that was counting the time he'd almost frozen to death rounding up strays during the bad winter about ten years back. Brad needed to end this ride and he needed to end it soon.

If it didn't, he was going to go way over the deep end. He didn't know what was wrong. Millie wasn't the kind of woman he should be thinking about dating. Who was he kidding? He'd stopped thinking about dating a mile back there and had gone right on to thinking of the big time.

He needed to end the ride. For one thing, she deserved someone more permanent than him. He wasn't ready for the *big* time. He was the kind of guy women looked to if they wanted a *good* time. And that was the way he liked it. He steered clear of women like Millie who made a man think of settling down and having babies.

He didn't know what was wrong. Millie didn't even wear lipstick, and yet he'd been one breath away from starting to whistle the wedding march. He barely knew the wedding march and, besides that, his lips were near frozen from the cold.

Brad shook his head. It must be something about the way she laid her cheek against his back that made him want to take care of her.

Of course, he knew it was only the Christmas craziness, but if he started whistling some wedding song, he'd make a fool of himself for sure.

"Yeah, we're almost there," Brad repeated himself as his horse walked into the edge of the ranch yard.

Millie thought she must be frozen to the back of Brad's saddle. "I can't move."

Brad had ridden into the barn and swung out of the saddle easily enough himself. But Millie was stuck. Her legs felt like they were permanently glued to the saddle.

The air was warmer inside the barn and the horse was standing politely beside the feed trough waiting to be given some oats. Randy and William had ridden over to the bunkhouse so they could unload the tree from the sled, but Brad and Millie had gone straight to the barn to dismount.

Millie tried to move her toes, and she felt the muscles tighten in her boots. At least she didn't have frostbite.

Brad took the reins of his horse and led the animal over to a small pile of hay. "You're just sore from all that riding. I didn't know we'd be gone that long."

"I'm never going riding again," Millie said, and then gave an exaggerated groan for emphasis.

Brad chuckled.

Oh, my word, Millie thought, *I almost made a joke. And he laughed.* She couldn't remember the last time she'd joked with a handsome man. Usually she only felt relaxed enough to joke with her women friends and men like Forrest who were shy themselves.

"It might help if you take the coat off," Brad said. "That'll help you move easier."

Millie pulled her left arm out of the parka and then finished pulling it off her right arm. She handed the coat down to Brad, and he set it on a hay bale. Millie shivered. It was cold, but she could move easier.

"Here," Brad said as he held his arms up to her. "Now let me swing you down, and you can sit on these bales."

Millie pushed against the back of Brad's saddle and tried to get her leg to properly swing itself over the horse. It didn't work. Finally, she just tilted her whole self over and let the leg come if it wanted.

Brad held his arms out to catch Millie. She fell into his arms and grabbed him around the neck. Usually when a woman had her arms around his neck, Brad recalled she also had a certain inviting look in her eyes.

Brad could only see one of Millie's eyes because he was actually facing her ear instead of her face, but he was pretty sure the look he hoped for wasn't there. Her eyes showed panic.

"Don't worry. I've got you," Brad whispered.

If it was possible, she looked even more alarmed.

"I can stand," Millie said.

Brad noted she didn't relax her grip on his neck, and her glasses were perched precariously on her nose.

"I think my leg just went to sleep, but it'll be fine when I put some weight on it," Millie added.

Since Millie wanted to stand, Brad shifted her, hoping to get her in a position where she could. He regretted it the minute he did it.

Instead of looking at her ear, Brad was now looking at those green eyes of hers. Both of them. Her glasses had fallen completely off, and he saw them resting on her shoulder. Without glasses, Millie's eyes went soft and dreamy. She relaxed in his arms.

Brad supposed Millie might have become calm

because she couldn't see, but he told himself it was just possible that it was because she was caught up in the magic of the moment, as he was—and that she was thinking how close they were to kissing, and if he just moved an inch or two this way and she moved an inch or two that way, they would meet in a kiss.

Brad took a deep breath just like the one he took every time he climbed into the chute at the Billings rodeo. He was an amateur at bull riding, just like he was an amateur at kissing. He'd never realized before, though, that a kiss could take every bit as much courage as climbing on the back of a two-thousand-pound bull.

"Oh," Millie said softly as Brad moved a little closer.

"May I?" Brad asked. He looked carefully at Millie's eyes. He didn't expect her to give him a verbal okay, but he did expect to see in her eyes if she was okay with a kiss.

"Oh," Millie repeated even softer.

Brad didn't see any refusal in her eyes. He looked twice to be sure. Then he took a deep breath and kissed her.

Millie thought her heart was going to stop. Failing that, her brain was going to melt. And it was all because her glasses had fallen off and in all the surrounding blur Brad was kissing her like he thought she was a fragile china doll.

Millie had been kissed before, but never like she was precious.

"Oh," Millie said when he pulled away a little bit.

Brad was smiling and, for some reason, he didn't look nearly as tall as he had before. It must be because his face was a little blurry and fuzzy. Millie decided she should go without her glasses more often if it made men like Brad look so very nice.

Millie heard the barn door open even though she couldn't actually see the door open. She could, however, see the big blocks of gray color that moved inside, and then she heard the neighing of a horse.

"Hey, there."

Millie recognized Randy's voice.

"What's happening here?" That was William. He sounded suspicious—like he'd added up the columns and wasn't sure they matched.

"I need my glasses," Millie said. If she was going to answer questions, she needed to be able to see.

Brad handed her the glasses.

"I was just helping Millie get off the horse," Brad said. His arms were still around Millie's shoulders.

William snorted. "Looked to me like you were helping her with a whole lot more than that."

Millie put her glasses on, and everything became clear. She could see through the open barn door that the night was almost fully dark now. The light Brad had turned on inside the barn gave the walls a yellow glow. Hay bales were stacked in one corner of the barn and horse stalls lined another wall.

William and Randy were both sitting on top of their horses and leaning forward as they looked at her and Brad. Randy was grinning, but William was looking stern and worried.

"My leg went to sleep," Millie explained. "I couldn't get off the horse, and Brad was helping me."

William looked directly at Millie. "You just be careful of him. He's a heartbreaker, he is."

"Oh." Millie blinked. Of course. She knew Brad was a flirt even if she had forgotten it for a moment. Men like him kissed women all the time for no good reason.

To be fair, women probably kissed Brad all the time for no good reason, too. He was certainly worth kissing if all of his kisses were like the last one. It wasn't his fault that Millie was the kind of woman who liked a reason for a kiss. A reason being maybe she was becoming a little special to the man kissing her.

Brad looked up at the other two ranch hands in astonishment. "Since when am I a heartbreaker?"

Brad always made very sure the women he was dating had no illusions about him. No one's heart had ever been cracked as far as he knew. Certainly, none had been broken. He didn't date the kind of woman who would be serious. "Besides, last night you were willing to let her sleep in my room with me because I was feeling a little down about Christmas. And now I can't kiss her!"

"That was different," William said firmly. "We didn't know Millie back then. Now, well—anyone can see she's the kind of woman who deserves a guy who's going to make a commitment."

Brad wanted to argue with that, but he couldn't. He didn't know much about Millie. He didn't even know for sure that she wasn't a thief or that she wouldn't leave tomorrow without saying goodbye. But one thing he did know: she did deserve one of those husbands mothers always wanted for their daughters. She deserved a man who could give her a home and financial security. Brad might have that someday, but today he didn't. He had nothing to offer a woman like Millie except his diesel pickup, and he had a feeling that wouldn't do.

"Well, then, we'd best get to the bunkhouse,"

Brad said. William sure knew how to bring a man down to earth. "It's cold enough out here to spit ice."

William nodded and smiled. "Charlie wasn't kidding about the cocoa. That'll warm you up. We could smell it when we took the tree inside."

Brad nodded. He supposed he would have to be content with that.

"Does he have marshmallows?" Millie asked.

Brad looked down at her. Her short blond hair was sticking out in all directions because she'd pulled off the wool cap he'd given her earlier. Her glasses were still a little crooked on her face. Her cheeks were red from the cold, and her lips were warm from his kiss.

Brad would have promised Millie the moon— the least he could do was get her some marshmallows. "If he doesn't, I'll go get some."

"Where?" William stopped midway through stepping down off his horse and turned to stare at Brad. "Where would you get marshmallows way out here in the middle of the night? And it's Sunday. Even the stores in Miles City are closed by now."

From the expression on William's face, Brad would have thought he'd offered to bring Millie the moon after all. "I could borrow some marshmallows from Mrs. Hargrove. She always keeps things like that on hand."

William finished stepping to the ground before he gave Brad another peculiar look.

"She's a well-prepared woman—Mrs. Hargrove is," Brad said for no reason other than to try and stop the look that was growing and growing on William's face.

"You don't have a temperature, do you?" William finally asked as he took a step closer to Brad. "I hear the flu this season makes people a little light-headed."

"I don't have a fever." Brad said. He couldn't swear that he wasn't light-headed, but he was pretty sure his temperature would log in at a normal 98.6 degrees.

"Well, we should get these horses taken care of and get inside anyway," William said. He gave Brad another curious look before he turned back to his horse. "No sense in hanging out here in the cold when we can be inside decorating the Christmas tree."

Brad nodded. He had forgotten about the Christmas tree. He had the whole Christmas thing yet to do. There would be the tree and more cinnamon on the stove. And that was only tonight. Tomorrow night would be Christmas Eve, and that would be even worse. He wondered if Charlie would want them all to go to the Christmas pageant at church. Brad had a feeling this was one holiday he would never forget.

At least when he thought of Christmas in the future, he could look back to this evening ride with Millie. If that wasn't Christmas magic, he didn't know what was.

Chapter Nine

The warm air in the bunkhouse made Millie's glasses fog up.

She stepped to the side of the doorway so that she wouldn't block the way as Brad and the other two men came inside the bunkhouse. The air inside smelled of chocolate and fresh pine. Empty cups ready for cocoa were sitting on a small table by one wall. The ranch hands were gathered around the small tree that was lying on the floor next to the black stove.

Millie rubbed her hands. The wood burning in the stove kept the large room heated. Her fingers had stung a little from the cold when she first stepped inside the room, but they were already starting to warm up. She was grateful for the prickly feeling in her hands as the heat reached them. That small tingling distracted her from The Kiss.

Millie stole a look up at Brad. He might be accustomed to a kiss like the one they had just shared, but she sure wasn't.

Brad was looking over at the group of men inside the room so Millie took her time and studied him carefully. He was handsome as usual. He still wore his hat, but she could see his face beneath it and it all looked normal. He wasn't wearing any tiny smile or dreamy expression on his face.

Millie frowned. She knew William had said Brad was a heartbreaker and she supposed she shouldn't be surprised that he didn't look any different, but she had secretly hoped he would. Not that she'd expected him to be smiling like an idiot or anything, but shouldn't he have some sort of funny look on his face after a kiss like that? He didn't look like he was affected at all. He certainly didn't have the stunned look she knew she was wearing.

She watched as Brad said a quick hello to the guys in the bunkhouse and then as he wiped his boots lightly on the rug by the door. He took his hat off and brushed the snow off it before he put it on a rack next to the door. He still had a few snowflakes melting on his cheek and his face was a little red from the cold.

Outside of that, Millie couldn't detect anything different about him. There was no sign Brad's heart had been beating in an irregular rhythm or that he was remembering a particularly sweet moment. In fact, he had paid more attention to his hat than he had to her since they'd come inside.

If Millie had been wearing a hat, she wouldn't even have remembered she had it on after that kiss. She felt like her own heart had been dipping and fluttering as if it belonged to a crazy woman. She'd even been trying to remember all she'd ever heard about flirting so that she'd know what to say next.

But now, seeing Brad, she hoped the sputtering happiness she felt inside hadn't shown on the outside. She was grateful she hadn't tried to say anything on the walk back to the bunkhouse. She didn't want to embarrass Brad by gushing over him when the kiss seemed like it was just routine to him. He probably kissed every woman who couldn't manage to get off a horse by herself. Maybe he meant it to be kind, like kissing backward children on the forehead to console them for their clumsiness.

Millie blinked and told herself it wasn't a tear that she felt in the corner of her eye. It was just moisture from the sudden heat of the room.

"I'm a little tired," she said as she gave a small yawn and an apologetic shrug. That should get rid of any doubt that she was still excited about a kiss that had happened a full five minutes ago. She didn't want anyone to think she was gullible enough to think that kiss mattered.

"Here, let me look at you," Brad said as he turned his full attention toward her. He bent his head and peered at her critically.

"I'm fine, though," Millie hastened to add. She didn't want to overplay being tired. Charlie would insist she go lie down, and she didn't want to miss any of this time taking a nap. Even if the kiss was nothing to remember, she wanted to remember every minute about this evening.

"How tired?" Brad asked as he took hold of her wrist and began to raise her hand up.

Millie blinked. Was he going to kiss her hand?

Brad stopped raising her hand and put his thumb on her wrist to feel her pulse.

"Being tired can be a sign you got too cold out there," he said. His blue eyes had deepened with worry. Millie started to hope maybe he did care, until he added. "People usually go to sleep just before they freeze to death."

"I wasn't that cold—and I'm not really that tired." Millie decided Brad was looking at her now like she was a sick bug at the bottom of a microscope. That wasn't the kind of attention she wanted. "I'm just—fine."

There had been many times in her life when Millie wished she were clever, but during none of those times did she wish it as fiercely as she did now. She felt as if she only knew how to flirt and be bold, she would know how to capture Brad's interest. Even a bug that knew how to flirt could capture his attention when he was standing so close.

Well, Millie guessed that technically she had his attention, but it was only because he thought she might be overly cold and on the verge of death. Brad probably didn't want to deal with the sheriff, which he'd have to do if he let her die while he was supposed to be watching her.

Unfortunately, all of the advice on flirting from other waitresses that she had listened to at Ruby's hadn't left her with a clue on how to flirt with a man when he was standing right in front of her counting out her pulse to make sure her heart was beating normally so she'd be able to pay for any crime she might have committed.

Of course, Millie thought optimistically, a woman didn't need to know how to flirt to be friendly. And the first step in being friendly was to find out more about the other person.

"You know, I never did get your last name," Millie said as she looked up at Brad. She smiled a little to show she was friendly, but not so much that he would think she was *too* friendly. It was the best she could do.

Brad looked down at Millie. She was smiling politely at him like she was a cashier at the grocery store and was asking him whether he wanted a plastic bag or a paper bag to carry home his potatoes. He had just kissed the woman. Shouldn't she at least look a little moved by the experience? "It's Parker. Brad Parker."

Millie nodded at him.

Brad expected her to ask about the weather next, and he didn't think he could hold his temper if she did. It was downright humbling to a man to know his kiss could have so little effect on a woman.

If he wasn't a little off-center because of everything that was going on, he would be able to think of something to say to make Millie smile at him like a woman ought to smile at a man who had just kissed her.

He could tell her that her eyes looked like emeralds when she laughed or that her skin was as soft as velvet, but Millie didn't look like the kind of woman who would like any of those words. Even he knew they were clichés. Unfortunately, in her case they were also true. Not that that would matter. Women always liked something that they hadn't heard before. Brad couldn't think of one thing to say that didn't sound like it had been said a thousand times already.

How did a man describe a woman like Millie?

"I see Charlie has the tree all ready to go," Brad said finally as he finished taking her pulse. "Your heart rate seems healthy."

At least her heart seemed to be doing better than *his,* Brad said to himself as he turned to face the other men in the bunkhouse, who were all gathered around the little tree they had chopped down.

Brad was glad none of the men were paying any attention to him and Millie. He suspected that wasn't because of good manners but because they'd finally gotten a steady look at the tree. It had been half dark when Randy cut it down, and sometimes things looked different when they had some light on them.

"It's kind of small," William said as he tipped the tree upright. The tree barely made it to William's belt buckle. "And it's got a bald spot where it didn't get enough sun. At least, I think that's its problem."

William turned the tree around so everyone could see the place where there were no branches.

"It's beautiful," Millie declared as she reached out and tried to coax a nearby branch into covering the bare spot. "It just needs a little help, that's all."

Millie didn't get the branch to cooperate and she stepped back.

"I guess we could stick it in the corner behind the lamp—if we angle it just right no one will see the bald spot," Charlie said hesitantly as he measured the tree with his hand. "And then maybe if we put some extra lights on it right there—"

"I only got one string of lights," Jeff interrupted as he handed a plastic bag to Charlie. Jeff had been leaning against the wall, but he stood up straight to deliver his lights. "And I was lucky to get those—the stores in Miles City are all sold out. Vicki at the grocery store had to get that strand from the back room. I owe her dinner some night next week."

Charlie reached into the bag and pulled the strand of lights out. He looked at them for a moment. "But these are pink."

Jeff nodded. "Well, Vicki said they were Easter lights—they used them around the store windows in April—but I figure lights are lights. There's no reason Christmas trees can't have pink lights."

There was silence for a moment.

"Maybe they'll turn sort of red when we get them on," Millie finally said. "Sometimes things look different when they're on a tree."

Brad didn't care if the lights were purple. Millie was looking at the tree the way he wanted her to look at him. "They'll look just fine. The thing is that they're lights."

Millie turned and looked at him gratefully. "That's right, and I've always liked lights."

Millie still wasn't looking at him with quite the adoration that she had for the tree, but Brad felt he was making progress. It was a sad day when he had to compete with a tree for the affection of a woman. Brad looked at the tree. To make it even worse that was one pathetic tree. He'd swear it had two bald spots instead of just one.

Brad reached up and patted his own hair just to reassure himself. It was damp, but all there. No bald spots for him.

"Did you get any ornaments?" Millie asked Jeff as she walked over to where the man stood.

Brad followed Millie over. He'd compete with the tree if he had to, but he wasn't about to compete with Jeff just because the man had a few fancy ornaments in his hand.

"Wait, let me get my camera," Charlie called out as he limped across the floor to the shelf on the wall. "I want to get pictures of the tree decorating from start to finish."

"Since when do you have a camera?" Brad asked.

Charlie never took pictures. Not even the time William rode the calf backward down the loading chute. Charlie always said a man should rely on his memory when it came to things he'd seen in his life.

"Jeff brought me back one of them box cameras—you know, they're made out of cardboard so if a cow steps on them or something you're not out a lot of money," Charlie explained as he picked up the disposable camera from the shelf. "I'm thinking of starting a Christmas memory scrapbook for the bunkhouse here."

Brad wasn't even stunned anymore. If the truth were told, he wasn't even listening. "That sounds nice."

Brad had stopped listening and just concentrated on looking. He wished he had a camera of his own, so he could take a picture of Millie. How did she manage to look twelve and twenty-three all at the same time? She had her head tilted to the side and was watching Jeff reach into the bag in front of him just like he was Santa Claus and the bag held the treasures of the world.

"Didn't your mother ever take you to see Santa?" Brad stepped a little closer so he could ask her the question and not risk it being heard by everyone in the room. He thought all mothers took their kids to see Santa Claus. He'd always imagined that, if his mother had lived, she would have taken him.

Millie looked up at him. Her eyes held on to the excitement of the tree as she shook her head. "I had a foster mother."

Somehow, Millie let him know all about her foster mother just by the flatness of her voice.

"I'm sorry." Brad was surprised by how much it disturbed him to know that someone had neglected Millie. She would have been the kind of little girl who should have had a mother who cared about her.

"It's all right," Millie said.

Brad scowled. No, it wasn't all right, but there was nothing he could do about it. Except perhaps get those ornaments for her. "If we need more things for the tree, I can drive to Billings tonight."

Charlie frowned and looked at his watch. "Even if the roads were good, the stores would be closed by the time you get there."

"They have that new place that's open twenty-four hours," Brad said. "What's it called—the something Mart?"

"Isn't that too far to drive?" Millie asked softly.

"It is when it's starting to snow like this." Charlie frowned again and shot Brad an incredulous look. "You've driven that road enough to know about that one place where it always drifts closed in a few hours after this kind of snow—now, I know you'd get to Billings, but you wouldn't get back before Christmas."

There was a moment of silence. Charlie stood holding his cardboard camera. He hadn't even taken one picture yet. William was still holding up the pathetic tree by its top branch. Jeff held the bag with whatever ornaments he'd found. Randy sat on the floor with a string of popcorn in front of him. They had all stopped what they were doing to look at Brad.

"Unless that's what you want," Charlie finally said quietly. "Not to be here for Christmas."

Brad was speechless. He had been ten kinds of a fool. Here he had spent years mourning the fact that he'd never had a family Christmas, and he'd had family who wanted to celebrate with him all that time. The guys in the bunkhouse weren't worried about his Christmas depression because it meant he wasn't his usual cheerful self. They were worried because they cared about him.

"There's no place I'd rather be for Christmas than right here with all of you," Brad said. His voice sounded heavy, so he gave a cough at the end of his speech. He wouldn't want anyone to think he was sentimental. It would be better if they thought he was coming down with something.

"Well, good then," Charlie said with a cough of his own. He set his camera down on a chair and pulled a big red handkerchief out of his jeans pocket to wipe at his eyes. "I think someone must have put some green wood in that stove—it's started to smoke a little and it's getting in my eyes."

"I don't see any—" Randy began, then stopped when William jabbed him in the ribs with an elbow. "Well, maybe a little smoke—"

Everyone was silent for a moment.

Finally, Millie spoke. "The tree doesn't really need decorations. It can still be a Christmas tree."

Brad could have hugged her for bringing them back to a safe topic.

"But I have some decorations," Jeff offered as he pulled a package of shiny red balls out of the plastic bag. There were six ornaments. "It might not be enough, but that's all they had left on the shelf."

"Well—" Charlie cleared his throat and put his handkerchief back in his pocket "—I don't want anyone worrying about decorations. I've been watching that television show, and that woman said you could make Christmas decorations out of anything you have around—old hair curlers or those cardboard things from toilet paper."

Randy frowned. "It doesn't seem right to have toilet paper on a Christmas tree."

"It's not the paper, it's the cardboard rolls."

"Oh." Randy still looked unconvinced. "I guess I just can't quite picture it."

"Well, do you have any old hair curlers lying around?" Charlie asked in exasperation.

Randy shook his head. "I guess toilet rolls are all right."

Everyone took a minute to look at the tree.

Brad was the first to hear the sound of a car— or maybe it was two cars—driving up to the bunkhouse. Charlie was the one who limped over to the window, however, and opened the curtains a little so he could see.

"Looks like we got company," Charlie announced. "Good thing I made lots of cocoa."

Millie walked over to the window, and Brad followed.

"Who'd be coming to see us?" Randy asked.

Brad had asked the same question. He knew every one of the men in the bunkhouse knew lots of people and went lots of places. But most of the places they went were bars, and the kind of people they met there weren't the type to come calling on a Sunday evening, especially when it was a long drive from the highway to the Elkton Ranch bunkhouse. When it was snowing, a person had to have a reason to come calling to the bunkhouse.

"Maybe it's Christmas carolers," Charlie said. "It looks like they've got a red light going—"

"It's the sheriff," Brad said. He doubted Sheriff Wall was coming to bring them a Christmas fruitcake.

Brad moved closer to Millie until he stood directly behind her as she looked out the window. The sheriff wouldn't be able to see Millie when he came in the door if Millie stayed right where she was. Brad knew he couldn't hide Millie from Sheriff Wall if she was wanted for a string of crimes, but that didn't stop him from wanting to try anyway. He told himself it was just because she was so little that he felt so protective of her. He didn't know why he had to get all mixed up with a woman who was probably a thief—and not a very good thief at that.

"What's the sheriff doing here?" Charlie said. Brad noticed the older man wasn't moving over to the door to open it.

"Maybe he found out something about Millie's money," William said with a frown. He wasn't moving toward the door, either.

No one was moving. Everyone just stood there worrying.

"Maybe it's not the sheriff," Jeff finally said. "Maybe he lent his car out to someone for the night and they got low on gas."

Brad snorted. "He wouldn't lend that car to his mother. No, he's here about the money."

"There's nothing he can say about the money," Millie protested softly. "It's just regular money."

Brad didn't even bother to answer her. There was nothing regular about a stack of hundred-dollar bills in this part of the country. He suspected there was nothing regular about it in Millie's life, either.

Chapter Ten

Millie had never seen so many silent men standing and looking at each other. Brad stood in front of her, and she wouldn't have even been able to see anything but his shirt if she hadn't moved to the side. She had no sooner moved than William stepped in front of her, and so all she saw was William's back.

Even Charlie, who had just opened the door, was still standing beside the open door like he was waiting for the sheriff to turn around and head back out of the bunkhouse. It took Charlie two minutes to close the door. By then the temperature inside the bunkhouse had fallen ten degrees.

Even when the door was closed, no one moved.

Finally, the sheriff spoke. "I thought I should check in."

He stood on the mat just inside the door, and the snow on his tennis shoes had not begun to melt. He hadn't smiled since he stepped inside. "Just doing my duty, you know."

No one answered.

"Well, you've checked in," Brad said finally.

Millie had never been a chatty waitress, but she knew that many fights had been avoided by a few friendly words, and sometimes it was as simple as finding a safe topic of conversation. She quietly stepped out from behind William and looked toward the sheriff. "Did you have an easy drive out from town?"

The sheriff turned to look at her. For her, he smiled. It was quick and humorless, but it was a smile. "Yes, I did."

Millie tried to smile back. "Good."

Brad shifted himself so he was in front of Millie again, but Millie didn't care. She had done what she could to start a regular conversation.

No one else offered any topics of conversation. Millie swore she could hear the frost growing on the windowpanes. Finally, she decided she needed to make one more attempt. She moved out from behind Brad again. "We've got a tree to decorate."

"I heard." The sheriff grunted. "That's why I'm here."

"You came to decorate our tree?" Brad asked in amazement.

Millie was glad she wasn't still standing behind Brad. She wouldn't have been able to see the astonishment on Brad's face if she had been. He was cute when he was dumbfounded.

"Not exactly," Sheriff Wall said. He finally took his cap off and held it in his hands. "I came to check out the story I heard that you rode horses back into the gullies to get the tree."

"Of course we rode horses," Brad said. "None of the pickups would have made it in all the snow back there."

The sheriff nodded. "I'm afraid I'll have to ask you to keep the barn locked then."

"What?"

Millie wasn't sure which of the men had asked that question. Maybe it didn't matter. They were all looking at the sheriff like he had forgotten where he was. Or maybe who he was.

"The barn doesn't have a lock," Charlie finally spoke.

"Oh," Sheriff Wall said as he looked at Millie and then studied the floor. "Well, then, I guess you'll just need to be sure that you keep a good eye on the—ah—the suspect so she doesn't steal a horse and ride out of here while she's under surveillance. I can keep an eye on the road through Dry Creek. But if she steals a horse and rides across the land, I'd miss her."

"Me?" Millie figured she was as astonished as the men now. "Steal a horse and ride it away? Across fields and everything?"

"She can't even get off a horse by herself," Randy said from the sidelines. "Probably can't get on one, either."

"She did just fine for a beginner," Brad said. "Nobody knows how to do anything the first time they try it."

"Me?" Millie still couldn't quite believe it. No one had ever accused her of doing something that adventurous before. "Do you really think I could do that?"

Brad figured he must have had a premonition about his life and that was why he never truly liked Christmas. People sure weren't themselves today, and the only thing that was different was that Christmas was the day after tomorrow. He couldn't believe Millie stood there looking at the sheriff like he had handed her a prize compliment.

"He's saying you would be running from the law," Brad said so she would understand there was nothing complimentary about it.

"Well, technically, it would be *riding* from the law," Sheriff Wall said. He'd stopped looking at the floor, and now, when he talked, he flashed a quick grin at Millie that made him look ten years younger.

Brad snorted. He could see the sheriff liked the look in Millie's eyes. She was looking at him like he had said something very clever. Brad would have been the first to congratulate Sheriff Wall if he had said something useful. But he hadn't. And it didn't matter how young he looked at the moment, the sheriff was too old for Millie.

"Could I learn how to ride a horse that quick?" Millie asked.

Brad started to feel uneasy. Millie looked a little too eager for his comfort.

"It's not about learning anything fast," Brad said. He looked at the sheriff. "You don't have to worry about Millie. Even if she knew how to ride a horse, she'd have more sense than to ride off by herself at this time of year across the fields. It's freezing out there."

"It's not so bad out," Sheriff Wall said as he started to take his jacket off. He still hadn't stopped grinning.

Brad frowned. He was finally getting a good look at the sheriff, and he was realizing what was wrong. He was wearing tennis shoes. That was part of the reason he looked so young. "What happened to your boots?"

"No sense in wearing them today in all the snow."

Brad snorted. "You've worn them in snowdrifts up to your hips. You're not wearing them now because they make you look taller—that's why. They add a good two inches to your height."

The sheriff shrugged. "There's nothing wrong with being short. I'm just being who I am."

Brad grunted. Who did Sheriff Wall think he was kidding? "I don't think many people are going to vote for a sheriff who doesn't wear boots."

"It's not election year for another two years."

"Time goes fast around here."

Millie figured Brad had that all wrong. Time didn't go fast at all. It fact it didn't even seem to crawl. It was frozen now that all the silence had come back.

"Maybe we should have some cocoa," Charlie finally said. He looked at the sheriff. "You're welcome to stay now that we know you've really come courting and not to make things difficult for Millie."

The sheriff looked like he was going to protest, but finally ducked his head in a nod. "Thanks."

"Courting!" Brad protested until Charlie cut in.

"A man's got a right to go courting," Charlie said firmly. "And the sheriff here is a good prospect for some woman. He's got a home—"

"He lives in the Collinses' basement," Brad said. "And that's only in the winter. I don't even know what he does in the summer when the water table rises and the basement's too damp."

"I'm looking around to buy a house," the sheriff said.

"And he's got a good public service job," Charlie continued, just as if Brad had not even spoken.

"A badge doesn't make a man any better," Brad said.

"I'm ready to get married," the sheriff said. "I'm not just looking for a good time, like some men."

Brad figured he was beat. Sheriff Wall was ready to make a commitment. Brad knew most mothers would look at a man like the sheriff and hope their daughters had sense enough to be interested.

Brad didn't like to be rushed. If he ever did get married, he wanted the marriage to be because he wanted to live with that particular woman and not because he had just arrived at some time in his life when he wanted a wife. But that kind of decision took time. The sheriff was as ready to marry as Brad was to date. Brad could never compete with Sheriff Wall if a woman was anxious to get married. And Millie, if she had any sense, would have to see that marriage to a man like the sheriff would solve all her problems.

Brad looked over at Millie. The smile on her face hadn't changed much since the sheriff started talking. Still, if she was smiling, that had to mean she was interested. Brad wondered if maybe he hadn't been too cautious about marriage in his life.

Millie didn't know why Brad had turned polite. He'd been arguing away with the best of them, and then he stopped and put a tight smile on his face and became quiet.

"Well, how many want cocoa?" Charlie said as he started walking to the small room off the back of the main room. That was Charlie's kitchen.

"I'd like some," Millie said. She turned toward Charlie. "And let me help you."

"No." Charlie shook his head. "You're our company, and the day I put company to work in the kitchen is the day that I retire as cook." Charlie looked around at the men in the room before looking back at Millie. "You sit and visit with the sheriff. Brad can help me."

Millie would have rather helped Charlie with the cocoa than sit and talk with a strange man. She didn't have anything in particular to say to the sheriff, especially since he had announced he was looking for a wife. He might be a little shorter than the other men in the room, but Millie couldn't picture herself being married to him all the same.

Of course, she still had to talk to him. The sheriff had walked over to the tree with her, and they were both looking at it.

"It's not always how big the tree is that counts," Millie remarked. That tree was looking shorter and shorter to her each time she saw it. She looked over at Randy. "You're not cutting more off the bottom, are you?"

"I'm not cutting anything off anywhere," Randy said.

"Maybe the branches are drooping when they thaw," William said as he walked over to look at the tree, too.

"Maybe we can set the stand on a box," Millie suggested. "I'm sure it'll look fine as long as it's up higher."

"And we don't have the decorations on it yet," Jeff chipped in as he carried his plastic bag over to the tree. He pulled out the string of lights again. "I tested these, and they're ready to go."

"But they're pink," the sheriff said as he looked at the lights. "Aren't you worried they'll make everything look a little strange?"

"The lights might look red when they're on the tree," Millie said. "You need to give them a chance."

Sheriff Wall looked at Millie. "You're right. That's the way we do it in Dry Creek. We always give everyone a chance."

Millie thought she might be turning a little pink herself. Not because she was embarrassed, but because she was annoyed. "You don't need to give me a chance. I didn't do anything wrong."

Brad held the mugs of cocoa a little higher. Good for Millie. She wasn't falling for the sheriff. She just stood there beside the tree looking a little fierce, like she was ready to defend something.

"Cocoa?" Brad offered one mug to Millie. "I put extra marshmallows in it for you."

Brad would have dumped the whole bag of miniature marshmallows in the cup if he could have. As it was, the melting tower of marshmallows only stood a half inch over the rim of the mug.

"Thanks." Millie took the cup and gave him a shy smile. "That's the way I like it."

Brad felt like he might be in the running after

all. Just to make sure, he added, "That tree is looking pretty good."

"Do you really think so?" Millie looked up at
him anxiously. "I'm hoping the decorations will
make it look better."

"We've only got six ornaments," Jeff reminded
everyone as he pulled one of the shiny red balls
from the bag. "There won't be enough to cover the
tree."

Everyone looked at the ornament Jeff held up.
It had a scratch on one side of the ball, and silver
showed through. The ornament was about two
inches in diameter and hung a little lopsided from
Jeff's fingers.

"I'll make some ornaments," Brad said. He regretted his words the minute they left his mouth.
How was he going to make ornaments? Then he
remembered a glimpse of a long-forgotten scene.
He was with his father, and his father was showing him how to make cowboy ornaments for the
Christmas tree. Brad must have been only four
years old at the time.

"You will?" Millie's face was lit up. "You'll
make ornaments?"

The look on Millie's face must have been what
his own face looked like all those years ago, Brad
thought.

"No one's getting me to make anything out of

toilet-paper rolls," Jeff muttered. "I don't care what they call those ornaments."

"And this popcorn has too many kernels to string right," Randy added. "I keep poking myself with the needle."

Brad kept looking down at Millie. "All we need is a whole bunch of empty tin cans."

Brad thought he was looking at the prettiest Christmas ornament there was. Millie's smile lit up her whole face, and Brad stopped noticing her glasses altogether. She was beautiful.

"That's one thing we've got is tin cans," Charlie said. He was holding two more mugs of cocoa and gave one each to Randy and Jeff. "We can empty more if we need them."

"We have some old paint in the barn, too." Brad was reluctant to stop looking at Millie, but he figured he'd better. He knew she didn't like a lot of attention coming her way, and he didn't want to spook her off just when he was beginning to think the two of them might have a chance.

"I'm planning to buy a farm in the spring," Brad said, only half realizing he had spoken his words instead of just thinking them.

Everyone turned to Brad and looked puzzled.

Brad cleared his throat. "I had thought some of that old paint might come in handy when I buy my place, but it's better to use what we can now."

Brad was relieved that his explanation seemed to make enough sense to everyone that they didn't pester him anymore about what he had meant. He wasn't ready to answer questions about anything. He hardly knew himself what the tumble of emotions inside of him was about. He was forgetting who he was. He was Brad Parker. He liked women who liked a good time. He wasn't the kind of a man to make a commitment.

Brad stopped for a moment. He'd forgotten the most important thing: Millie. He didn't know much about her, but he did know that she hadn't had an easy life. She deserved a man who was better than Brad Parker and the sheriff combined. She deserved to marry a saint.

Brad looked at her. Everyone in the room had turned their attention back to the Christmas tree. Millie was frowning slightly at it.

"Maybe if we just move this branch," she finally said as she reached out and gently bent one of the branches.

Brad knew the tree was a hopeless cause. He also knew that it was a cause that was important to Millie. He might not be saint enough to marry her, but he sure could do his best with that tree of hers. "I've got some twine we can use if we need it."

Millie smiled gratefully up at him. "Do you think it will work?"

Brad nodded his head. He'd make it work even if he had to nail more branches on that tree. He was going to give Millie a good Christmas if he had to use every nail and tin can on the Elkton ranch.

Chapter Eleven

Millie let go of the sigh she was carrying. Randy had tied his picture angel to the top of the tree, and Charlie had turned off the last of the lamps in the bunkhouse. Everyone was standing in a circle around the tree. Millie decided there was no doubt the scraggly pine was a Christmas tree now that it was all dressed up.

Brad had used a hammer and a nail to pound holes into the sides of dozens of tin cans, and when he put a small candle in the middle of each tin, the candlelight shone through the holes and made hundreds of tiny twinkling stars. The cans themselves had been painted dark red, and some of them had white trim.

Jeff and William had tied the cans to the tree with haying twine before adding the decorations

Jeff had bought. The strand of pink lights circled the tree a couple of times, and with the red of the tin cans, the lights actually looked like they belonged.

"It's beautiful," Millie said.

Brad let go of the sigh he was carrying. It had occurred to him when he was halfway through emptying out all of the soup cans in the kitchen that the tree would look homemade with the ornaments he was making. Tin cans couldn't really compete with ornaments a person could buy in the store. He didn't want Millie to be disappointed in the tree. If it wasn't too late to get to Billings and back, he would have dug his way past the drift that usually stopped people and gone out to buy more ornaments right then. Even now he wasn't sure. "You really like it?"

Brad wondered how it could be that, with five other men hovering around the tree, Millie smiled up at him like those tin cans were filled with diamonds instead of holes and it was all due to him.

"It's just like I've always pictured a Christmas tree should look," Millie said softly. "It reminds me of a starry night."

Brad swallowed. The light from the candles flickered over Millie's face in the darkness and then left her in shadow. "I'm glad you like it."

The other men were silent except for the

sounds of swallowing or coughing or clearing their throats. Charlie was the only one brave enough to bring out his handkerchief and dab at his eyes.

"That smoke's still hanging around," Charlie muttered after he put his handkerchief back into the pocket of his overalls.

Each of the men had their faces turned toward the Christmas tree. The tree itself was standing on a wooden crate that Jeff had pulled in from the barn. Charlie had donated a few white dishtowels to cover the tree stand and the crate. Millie had arranged the towels so they looked almost like snow-drifts.

The clock was ticking in the corner of the room, and the fire was crackling a little as it burned in the corner stove, but otherwise it was a silent night.

"It's too bad Mrs. Hargrove isn't here," William said finally. "She'd have us all singing a carol or two—"

Brad wished the older woman were here with them. She'd enjoy the tree.

"Oh, that reminds me," the sheriff said as his hand went to his shirt pocket. Sheriff Wall was wearing a white shirt with broad gray stripes and a black leather vest. "She asked me to give you something when she heard I was coming out here tonight."

The sheriff pulled several blue index cards with printing on them out of his shirt pocket. "These are the visitor forms for the church. In all the commotion, she forgot to have you fill them out this morning, and she felt bad about it."

Charlie frowned. "I didn't know you had to fill out a form to go to church. Is it like voter registration?"

"Nah," Sheriff Wall said as he fanned the cards out and held them out to everyone. "It's just a new program Mrs. Hargrove volunteered to do. I don't really know much about it—I've only gone to church the past month or so, and they didn't have them back then. I think it's just to give Mrs. Hargrove your address or something so she can send you another postcard."

"Mrs. Hargrove knows where we live," Charlie said, but he took one of the cards anyway. "Still, I guess it's only polite to thank the church for having us, so I guess I'll be filling one out."

After Charlie took a card, he gave a stern look to those around him. Finally, William took a card. Then Randy and Jeff each took one. Brad held his breath when he put his hand out and took one. Millie even took one.

Everyone just looked at his or her card.

"Mrs. Hargrove said something about handing them back to her when Millie comes to town tomorrow to do her community service," the sheriff said. He looked pleased with himself that he had delivered all of the cards. "I'll be happy to come by tomorrow and pick Millie up so she can get started."

"Millie and I will be in town at eight," Brad said. He put the card in his shirt pocket. He was perfectly able to see to Millie. "There's no need for you to drive all the way out here."

"I don't mind," the sheriff said before he shrugged his shoulders and looked at Brad. "Don't suppose it matters, though—I will see you and Millie at eight. I thought maybe we should meet in the café."

"I thought we were going to the church," Millie said. "To take care of the black marks on the floor."

"We'll start out at the café," the sheriff said as he walked toward the closet that held his coat. "We'll be wanting some coffee and the county runs a tab there. Linda showed me where everything was before she left—even her flavored creamers."

"Linda trusted you with the stuff in her café?" Charlie asked. The older man was frowning.

"Yeah," Sheriff Wall said as he opened the closet door and reached for his coat. "Of course she trusts me. I'm sworn to uphold the law."

"That wouldn't have made any difference to Linda a year or so ago," Charlie commented as he walked over to the door. "I guess she's finally growing up. She always struck me as someone who'd rather put poison in a lawman's coffee than creamer. I don't suppose she sits down with you while you drink it, though, does she?"

The sheriff grinned. "Now that you mention it, she does. I guess we all grow up sooner or later."

Sheriff Wall he put his coat on and walked toward the door before turning to the others in the room. "We'll see some of you tomorrow."

Millie smiled. "We'll be there."

"I'll wish the rest of you a Merry Christmas then," the sheriff said as he tipped his hat to the group. "Be sure and watch that tree of yours, or you'll burn the bunkhouse down."

"We'll be fine," Brad said. He had seen the flicker of worry in Millie's eyes. "There's enough snow outside to stop a forest fire anyway."

"That's true," Millie said.

Brad didn't bother to wave to the sheriff as the man opened the door and stepped into the night darkness. Sheriff Wall could find his way home all right. Brad was much more interested in Millie.

"I could bring some snow in if you're worried," he offered. He figured the candles would burn for another half hour or so. He wanted Millie relaxed while she watched it. "Just so it's handy if we need it for anything."

Millie was happy. She was having the kind of Norman Rockwell Christmas that she'd imagined. Granted, Christmas Eve wasn't until tomorrow, but she was sitting here with a group of people who had actually decorated a tree.

Millie had always known she could decorate a tree for herself when she was in Seattle. One year she'd even bought some tinsel and lights. But when it came time to get a tree, she didn't. Part of her Christmas dream was to decorate a tree with other people.

"We've got more cocoa," Charlie said as he sat down on one of the leather couches that Jeff had pulled closer to the tree. "It's self-serve in the kitchen."

Millie walked over and sat down on the couch next to Charlie. "You make great cocoa."

Charlie beamed as though she'd handed him a hundred-dollar bill. For the first time that night, Millie remembered what she was doing in Dry Creek. She had a mission, and it had nothing to do with tin-can lights and cocoa.

Millie looked around the room. She didn't feel like a stranger anymore. She wondered how she could fulfill Forrest's request or if it was really necessary.

"The community service won't be hard," Brad said as he sat down on the couch next to Millie. "No one really expects you to work."

Millie had to stop herself from scooting over to sit pressed against Brad.

"*I* expect me to work," Millie said. Her voice was a little sterner than she had intended. She didn't care what Sheriff Wall thought about her and her community service, but Millie hadn't been a slacker before she came to Dry Creek, so there was no reason to start now.

Brad smiled slightly. "I guess I'm not surprised at that."

"We can't all be prima donnas," Millie continued. She didn't want Brad to think she was boring, but she just couldn't summon up the effort to pretend to be carefree. She was a person who obeyed the rules in life, and that was just the way it was.

Brad smiled wider. "No chance of that happening. You won't even let me wait on you."

"You got me cocoa," Millie protested. She wasn't used to a man wanting to help her with her coat and that kind of thing. She was used to doing this for herself *and* a table of other people at the same time. "Besides, I don't need help with much."

Brad stopped smiling. "I scared you with all my talk of spiders before. I'm sorry I did that."

Millie didn't know who had moved, but she was sitting closer to Brad on the sofa than she had been before. She looked around the room. Charlie had gotten up from the sofa and was over by the table. Jeff and Randy had left the room, and she could hear them in the kitchen. William alone sat near the tree. If Brad only knew, it wasn't spiders she was scared of right now.

"It's okay," Millie said as she tried to move away from Brad without being obvious about it. She was afraid she had been the one to move closer in the first place, and she didn't want him to think she was—

"Oh." Millie realized that as she moved away, Brad moved closer. Maybe she wasn't the one who had moved on the sofa after all.

William got up and left his place beside the tree. Millie looked around. She and Brad were alone in the room. "Everyone's in the kitchen."

"Probably more cocoa." Brad doubted it was a sudden thirst for cocoa that had made the other men give them some privacy, but Brad was glad for the kindness they were showing him.

He wasn't sure if it was good news or bad news that Millie looked so nervous around him all of a sudden. He wished he had another month or two to get to know her before he kissed her again. But he didn't have a month. She would be gone by then for sure. He tried to slide down into the sofa cushions a little more. Maybe she really *didn't* like tall men.

Brad pulled the blue form out of his shirt pocket, more for something to do than because he even remembered what the form was for.

"I wonder what they send you," Millie said. She was looking down at her own form intently.

The Welcome Visitors form was as basic as they came, Brad figured, but he was grateful for it. Even with all of the lamps in the room off, there was enough light from the tree to see what was on the card. There was a graphic of a church on one corner and several printed questions in the middle of the card. One question asked if you would like someone from the church to visit you. The other asked if you had a prayer request. At the bottom, the church said they'd send a special gift to anyone who returned the card with his or her address. That must be what Millie had just read.

"It can't be much," Brad said. "The church doesn't have money to buy people anything. They've been raising money for the past year just to get a new organ for the place."

"Money's tight around here, isn't it?"

"Not so tight that we don't get by," Brad said. He didn't want Millie to think they were poor in

Dry Creek. "And when money *is* tight—or someone has a health problem or something—we all chip in and help them over the hump."

Brad wished he'd paid more attention to the accountant he'd paid to do his taxes last year. Brad was so close to having enough to buy a place of his own that he had wanted to ask the man a few questions about buying property in addition to the usual questions about his taxes. "We're not rich by any means, but no one has lost their place or not had enough for some medical care—at least, no one that I've known of, and I've lived here for ten years."

"You mean you haven't always lived here?" Millie asked.

Brad could swear she was surprised. He tried real hard not to be offended. He knew some women put great stock in men who had traveled and been lots of places. Some of the waitresses he'd known thought travel was the measure of a man. Of course, that might be because they were used to truckers, and a trucker wasn't really a trucker until he'd been to both coasts a few times. But Brad had never had any desire to move around.

"I was born in Illinois," Brad said, "but I like Dry Creek. I don't expect I'll be moving from here."

"But surely you travel?" Millie insisted.

"Not if I don't have to," Brad said. He figured the woman might as well know him. He was a basic kind of a guy. No particular flash. He wasn't one to fly a woman over to Paris for her birthday. Now, he *might* drive her to the coast or up to Canada for a long weekend or something.

Millie didn't seem to have anything to say in response to him not traveling so Brad just sat there on the sofa. He figured his chances were about zero.

"Does anyone in Dry Creek travel?" Millie asked. She was suddenly realizing that she would need to leave in a couple of days. After she completed her community service, there would be no reason to stay in Dry Creek. And she couldn't stay. Once she gave out her Christmas presents, she would be broke. She'd have to go back to work. She accepted that, but she'd hoped that she might see some of the people in Dry Creek again. She'd hoped at least some of them occasionally went to Seattle.

"Mrs. Hargrove flew up to Alaska to see Doris June a couple of years ago," Brad said. "She liked the moose—they walked right down the streets in Anchorage just like they owned the place."

"Does anyone else go anywhere?"

Brad was silent a minute. "The sheriff goes to

conventions every year—he gets around pretty good."

"Oh." Millie blinked and looked down at the card in her hand so that Brad wouldn't see the tears in her eyes. She supposed she was silly to have gotten so attached to the people in this town. Millie looked out of the corner of her eye at Brad. He was sitting a little awkwardly, like he was trying to push himself into the sofa cushions. He had a frown on his face, and he was staring straight ahead at the tree. But Millie wished he was the one who went to conventions. If he went to conventions, he was bound to come to Seattle once in a while.

"I went to a rodeo once," Brad offered.

"Really? Where?"

"Cheyenne."

"Oh." Millie realized that she had never heard of anyone having a rodeo in Seattle.

Brad swore he didn't know how to please a woman. He'd finally realized he could offer a wife some excitement, and Millie sat there looking like it was nothing to her. Of course, he supposed it didn't matter to her where he took any future wife. "Rodeos can be good entertainment."

Millie nodded. "Now that I know more about riding a horse, I can appreciate them more."

Her response certainly didn't ring with enthusiasm. Brad figured he could have suggested a trip to the dentist and gotten the same response. He told himself it was probably just as well. If excitement and travel were important to Millie, it was good that he knew it now.

"I should have gone and gotten some better decorations for the tree," Brad said. The poor thing looked a little forlorn to him just now, even though the candles were all still burning brightly and he had arranged branches so that he'd covered the bald spots on the tree. Why had he thought that tin-can ornaments could compete with the shiny new balls that people expected on their trees these days?

"I love that tree," Millie said fiercely.

"Really?"

Millie nodded firmly. "It's beautiful."

"Yes," Brad agreed, even though he'd stopped watching the tree and was watching Millie watch the tree. The candlelight reflected off her glasses and cast a golden glow all over her face. When had her face become the only one he wanted to look at? Her hair still didn't have any more brass in it, and she still didn't wear any of the makeup that he'd thought looked so good on most women. But she was beautiful.

Brad moved a little closer on the sofa. Millie didn't move away. He took that as a sign of encouragement and moved closer still. Millie did look up at him when he did that. But she didn't move away. Instead, she gave him a shy smile.

Brad moved all the way closer and put his arm on the sofa behind Millie.

Millie forgot about how much she would miss Brad when she left. She forgot about the fact that she was a cautious woman and not at all the kind of woman men like Brad wanted to date. All she could think about was the moment she was living.

Brad had his arm around her, and they were looking at the most beautiful Christmas tree she had ever seen. The light from the candles danced between the pine branches of the tree and reflected off the bottoms of the tin cans. The pink lights added a softness to the shadows the branches cast.

Millie was having her Christmas. The Norman Rockwell one Forrest had wanted her to have.

"I owe him an apology," Millie spoke without thinking.

"Who?" Brad said as he moved his arm from the back of the sofa to her shoulders.

Millie felt enclosed and happy. "Just a friend."

Millie took a good look around her. She wanted to remember this Christmas for the rest of her life. She hoped she'd remember the feel of Brad's arm around her as well as the flickering light of the candles on the Christmas tree. She'd never experienced anything like it yet in her life, and she wasn't hopeful enough to expect another one to come along. But she sure would be grateful if it ever did.

Chapter Twelve

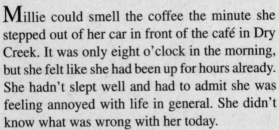

Millie could smell the coffee the minute she stepped out of her car in front of the café in Dry Creek. It was only eight o'clock in the morning, but she felt like she had been up for hours already. She hadn't slept well and had to admit she was feeling annoyed with life in general. She didn't know what was wrong with her today.

Well, maybe she did know, she thought as she shut her car door. But there was nothing to be done about it. Last night had shown her what Christmas was all about, and the experience had made her feel more alone than she'd ever felt in her life.

No wonder her foster mother had never bothered with Christmas.

A sentimental Christmas wasn't worth it when

a person had to go back to her real life. And for her, Millie thought, real life consisted of waiting on tables of complaining, demanding people at Ruby's cafe.

"I guess the sheriff is here."

Millie looked up at Brad when he spoke. He had driven behind her into Dry Creek after she had refused his offer to ride in his pickup with him. For some reason, she wanted to be alone in her old car. She certainly didn't want to be sitting next to Brad. The wind made his lips white and his face red, but he didn't seem in any hurry to step past her and go into the café.

The morning itself was dreary. The sun was hidden behind thick gray clouds, which probably meant snow was coming later today. The snow that had fallen yesterday was tramped down around the café and didn't look as clean as it had yesterday. A film of dirt had settled over everything.

"I hate snow," Millie announced.

Brad only grunted. "Everybody can't live at the beach."

"I don't live at the beach," Millie protested. She rented a small apartment so close to the docks that she perpetually smelled fish. She tried hard to convince herself the neighborhood was charming. "It's the waterfront, and that's altogether different."

Now that Millie thought about it, she didn't know what she had against snow. The weather on the docks in Seattle could be just as wet and almost as cold as Montana in winter. Maybe she had just always hated snow because it reminded her of all those days she'd spent with her foster family in Minnesota. She had moved to Seattle five years ago to start a new life. Some days, though, it felt like her new life was just a repeat of her old life. All that had changed were the people sitting around the tables that she waited on.

"It's all by the water," Brad said. His lips were pressed into a line that could not be mistaken for even the smallest of smiles. "I know there's fancy prices at the coast, but living by the water doesn't make a man a better man. There's nothing wrong with a bit of snow. Lots of good men live in the snow."

Millie didn't have a chance to answer because Brad started walking up the steps to the café. His boots stomped on each step, one at a time, until he reached the top.

Brad figured he had ruined any chance he'd ever had with Millie. But, he said to himself as he opened the door, it was probably just as well. There was no point in imagining how much fun he and Millie would have on a real date when he knew the price he'd have to pay when she left. The simple fact was, they had no future and he was wise to realize that.

Brad stood to the side and held the door for Millie.

He smelled cinnamon on her when she walked by. Millie had helped Charlie prepare an early breakfast this morning, and Brad couldn't help but notice she had been not only civil, but downright nice to Charlie. In fact, Millie had had a smile for all of the men in the bunkhouse…except for him.

Brad wondered when everything had changed with him and Millie. She'd seemed to like his arm around her last night. She had even snuggled up against him the little while they sat and looked at that tree.

It was the tree's fault, Brad decided. No good ever came from taking a pathetic little pine tree and dressing it up like it was something to stare at. It gave rise to all kinds of hopes in a man's chest that just simply weren't going to come true. Maybe there was a good reason he'd never liked Christmas, Brad told himself as he followed Millie into the café. Maybe he didn't like Christmas because he had the sense to be content with his lot in life and wasn't given to empty dreaming.

Christmas was nothing but a promise that hadn't come true in his life. Maybe it did for some people, but it hadn't for him.

"Good morning," the sheriff called out in greeting to Brad and Millie, just as if he were blind and not able to see they were miserable. "Looks like it'll be a good day."

"It's overcast," Brad said. "It'll probably snow later, unless it's too warm to snow—then it'll be some kind of icy slush."

Brad didn't know how any man could be optimistic with the thought of slush falling on him later in the day, though the sheriff seemed like he could be. At least he didn't flinch when Brad informed him of the prospect.

"I got the coffee ready for you, but I'm going to need to go into Miles City. I have some official work to get done," Sheriff Wall said as he started to put his coat back on.

Brad could see that several cups, napkins and spoons had been set out on one of the tables. Someone had even folded the napkins, and Brad was sure it hadn't been the café owner, Linda, because the corners were all crooked. When Linda bothered to fold napkins, she got them straight.

"Thanks," Brad said, even though he figured the sheriff wasn't listening to him since he was looking at Millie. Sheriff Wall was as pathetic as he was, Brad figured by looking at him. Maybe the sheriff was worse, Brad decided. At least Brad hadn't tried folding napkins to impress Millie.

"Did you sleep all right last night?" the sheriff asked Millie just as though he cared.

Millie nodded. Brad had to give her points for knowing to be cautious about the sheriff. Of course, he then took some points away when she smiled at Sheriff Wall as she said thank-you. A simple thank-you would have been enough. She didn't need to smile at the man. The lawman would be out folding more than napkins if Millie didn't tone down those smiles.

"I'll be back in a few hours," the sheriff continued. "Might even make it back for lunch. Mrs. Hargrove promised to make us her special meat loaf with black olives—it's her Christmas special."

Millie longed with all her heart to have a special Christmas recipe that people knew about. Since she usually worked on all of the holidays, her Christmas special was whatever the chef had made for the day. And the only reason people asked her for it was because she was their waitress. Most of them didn't even know her name.

"Maybe I'll ask for her recipe—unless it's a secret." Millie looked at Brad. "Do you think it's a secret?"

"I doubt it. It's hard to keep anything a secret in Dry Creek."

Millie didn't point out that *she* still had a secret. Maybe that's why she was feeling so cranky today. She had a secret and she didn't want to keep it a secret. She wanted to tell Brad what she was doing and why she was in Dry Creek.

"Well, I guess I better get going," the sheriff said as he nodded his head at Millie. "Besides, I see Mrs. Hargrove coming, so you guys will be getting down to work in no time."

Millie smiled goodbye to the sheriff. She guessed the spilling of secrets would have to wait until she got the floors in the church all scrubbed.

Thinking of the floors made Millie feel more cheerful. There was nothing like getting rid of black marks to make a person feel like they had accomplished something in a day. She might not have a special Christmas recipe, but she did have a special cleaning method.

"Aren't you worried about what she's going to put on those floors?" Brad asked the sheriff, just to remind the man that it hadn't been that long ago that he thought Millie was planning some kind of a crime. The sheriff had made that remark about the water supply and hadn't followed up. Brad wondered what kind of a lawman the sheriff was.

"Naw," the sheriff said as he waved goodbye. "I ran her through the system and got enough information on her to put my mind at ease. Besides, I have a buddy on the Seattle police force."

"Does that mean I don't have to do the floors?" Millie asked.

The sheriff stopped with his hand on the door. "Well, you still broke into the place…"

Brad held his breath. If Millie didn't have to do the floors, she didn't have to stay at all. He thought he at least had today to convince her to stay. He was glad she had the community service. If there was one thing he knew about Millie, it was that she didn't take the easy road anywhere.

Millie nodded. "I would do them anyway. I just wanted to know if anything was going on my official record."

The sheriff went a little pink at this.

"Don't worry," Brad said. "Unless I miss my guess, the sheriff didn't even file the report. He hates paperwork."

Sheriff Wall left the café as Mrs. Hargrove entered it, and they nodded to each other.

"Good, the coffee's on," the older woman said as she unwound a wool scarf that she'd worn around her head. "There's nothing like a cup of coffee to get me going in the morning."

Mrs. Hargrove drank her cup of coffee while she was standing on the welcome mat in the front of the café. "I got snow on my boots coming over here, and I don't want to track up this clean floor.

We have enough to do with getting one floor clean. No point in adding another floor to the list."

Millie looked at Mrs. Hargrove. She was wearing a navy parka over a pink gingham dress. Forrest had told Millie that Mrs. Hargrove usually wore a gingham dress in some color or another.

"You don't want to get your dress dirty," Millie said. "Brad and I brought lots of old clothes if you'd like to borrow some."

When Millie left the bunkhouse, Charlie had insisted on giving her old flannel shirts to take with her and several pairs of men's overalls.

"They're full of holes," Charlie had said when he handed the two bags to Millie. "So you might want to wear a couple of the shirts at the same time—mostly the holes aren't in the same places."

Millie looked at the older woman. "I've got the old clothes in the trunk of my car. I thought I'd take them over to the church and put them on there."

"Makes sense, since the church is heated. Pastor Matthew said he went over and turned the heat on at seven this morning, so it should be comfortable by now. And don't you worry about these dresses of mine—they all wash up fine," Mrs. Hargrove said. "I haven't met the stain yet that I couldn't figure out—except for the black marks on the church's floor. I'm anxious to see how this baking soda idea of yours works."

"Oh," Millie remembered. "The sheriff didn't leave me the box of baking soda he said he had in his office."

"Don't worry," Mrs. Hargrove said as she patted the pocket of her parka. "I brought a small box that I had. It's brand-new—never been opened. Don't know if that makes a difference or not, but I'm not taking any chances. Those black marks have been bothering me for years now."

Millie knew how easily water splashed, and that was why she had worried about Mrs. Hargrove's clothing. She'd never once expected the woman to help her clean the floor. But it was clear when she, Brad and Mrs. Hargrove walked up the steps of the church ten minutes later that the older woman expected to scrub.

"Oh, no," Millie said as she took the final step up to the church. She had her purse strapped around her neck, and her hands were free. Her long wool coat kept her warm even though the air was cold. Millie stopped to take a breath. "You don't need to get down on your knees or anything. There's plenty of cleaning you can do without that."

"Maybe you could dust the rails of some of the pews," Brad suggested. He had carried up both bags of old clothes even though Millie had protested.

"You mean sit down while the real work is going on?" Mrs. Hargrove asked as she turned the doorknob on the church's outer door. "Nothing ever got cleaned by someone sitting down and taking a swipe at a little bit of dust. Besides, the pews will be cleaned later this morning. The twins do that when it's the Curtis family's turn at cleaning. I think they pretend the pews are dragons."

Millie knew the twins liked dragons. What she didn't know was that they cleaned the church. "Aren't they too young?"

"Too young. Too old," Mrs. Hargrove said as they stepped into the church. "Sometimes it seems that all of the work at the church is being done by the people you wouldn't expect."

Millie and Brad followed Mrs. Hargrove into the church.

"Of course, that's the beauty of it," Mrs. Hargrove said as she stood in the entryway to the church and unwound the scarf from her head again. "The Bible talks about the weak being made strong and the slave being made free. I figure that since the very beginning, the church has been surprised by what people can do and be."

"But that was a long time ago, wasn't it? The beginning, that is." Millie was remembering the time when she'd gone to church with her foster mother and the woman had told her that Jesus lived thousands of years ago and so had no meaning for today.

Mrs. Hargrove shrugged her shoulders. "God says a thousand years are but a day to Him. The way I see it, we're still in the early days with God and will be for a long time at that rate."

"You said there were scrub brushes around?" Brad asked. Just because God had all day didn't mean Brad did. He figured if he got the floor cleaned in the church before lunch, then maybe Millie would agree to go riding horseback again with him this afternoon. If he could get her leaning into him on the horse again, maybe he could talk to her and he could ask her to stay in Dry Creek for a little longer.

Brad decided he needed his head examined. Women didn't just stay in Dry Creek while they waited for some man to get to know them. No, he needed a better plan than that.

"Brad?" Millie asked for the second time. Brad was standing there, muttering to himself and frowning. He hadn't even heard her the first time she said his name.

"Huh?"

Brad focused on her, but she couldn't help but notice that his face turned a little pink at the same time.

"Mrs. Hargrove said the brushes are on the

shelf above the sink in the kitchen. Do you know where that is?"

"Yeah, sure," Brad said as he started to walk toward the small room on the side of the church. "I was just going to get them."

When Brad stepped into the kitchen, Millie turned to Mrs. Hargrove. "I hope he's okay."

The older woman chuckled. "Oh, he's okay, all right."

"He seems a little distracted."

The older woman chuckled even harder. "I'd say that's a fair bet."

Millie frowned. She'd hoped to have another conversation with Brad like the one she'd had yesterday, and that didn't seem too likely if he was going to be distracted by something as simple as brushes.

"Is there a restroom where I can change?"

"Right through there, dear. The second door on your left."

Millie ended up wearing two flannel shirts and one of Charlie's old coveralls. She needed some twine to belt the overalls tight to her waist so they didn't flap around too much, but outside of that, everything had adjusted to her.

Millie decided it was a good thing she'd changed when she first got to the church. If she'd waited ten minutes, she never would have changed. That's when Pastor Matthew and his two boys came over to the church.

Millie had already started to scrub the first black mark. If she hadn't already been on her knees, the sight of Pastor Matthew would have put her there.

The minister wore an apron. Well, maybe it wasn't so much an apron as it was a dishtowel tied around his waist. But Millie could hardly believe what she was seeing. "He's going to start cleaning."

"I thought I told you it was the Curtis family's turn to clean the church this week," Mrs. Hargrove said. The older woman was sitting on one of the pews near Millie sorting through a box of crayons from one of the Sunday School classrooms. She had finally agreed to observe instead of scrub, since there were only two scrub brushes and Brad insisted he was going to take one and scrub beside Millie.

Millie had her scrub brush in one hand and water stains on her overalls. She'd clipped her hair back as best she could with the barrettes she had in her purse. She still couldn't believe it when she saw Pastor Matthew go into the kitchen with a mop. "But he's the minister!"

"I hope you're not saying that men can't scrub floors," Brad said. Millie looked over at him. He had speckles of black on his face and his forehead was damp. He had been working on some black marks about ten feet away from her, and Millie had to admit he was doing a good job.

"Well, ah, no, I wasn't saying that exactly." Millie wondered what she *had* been meaning to say. Of course, she knew that some men worked at cleaning. She'd seen janitors before. But, somehow, even with the janitors, she'd always assumed that they never cleaned or helped out at home.

"I'm just surprised that a minister would be doing the cleaning," Millie finally said. "Isn't he the boss?"

Mrs. Hargrove chuckled. "He'd be the first to tell you that he's not."

Millie couldn't figure it all out.

"When was the last time you did this?" Millie demanded as she sat back and looked straight at Brad. Even he must not clean regularly.

Brad stopped scrubbing. "Me?"

Millie nodded.

"I've never done this before," Brad said.

Ah, Millie thought to herself, she was right.

"At least not here," Brad continued. "But I do my share of cleaning up after other people. Just ask Charlie. We all take turns."

Millie frowned. This isn't what she expected. But even if Brad was willing to clean something on occasion, that didn't explain why the minister would.

"I thought ministers told people what to do," Millie said finally. She was puzzled. She had always thought that getting close to God would mean that she'd be run ragged doing errands for Him. He was powerful and He was male. That meant there would be no end to doing things for Him. "He should tell somebody to scrub the floor."

Mrs. Hargrove nodded. "I know it seems like that's the way it would work. But God has turned everything upside down."

Millie felt like she was the one who'd been turned upside down. Why would someone who could order others around do anything? "And where's Glory?"

"I think she's painting a scene for the pageant," Mrs. Hargrove said as she put the blue crayons in a plastic bag and tied a knot in the bag. "Everyone decided to try a simpler pageant this year, but we still wanted it to be nice."

Millie wasn't so sure she wanted to talk about God, but she wanted to talk about the Christmas pageant even less. It seemed like every time anyone brought up the Christmas pageant, they also brought up Forrest. When Millie thought of Forrest, she remembered those Christmas stockings in her trunk and wondered if she'd ever be able to fulfill Forrest's final request.

"But who does all the praying if the minister scrubs the floor?" Millie asked. She remembered the blue card in her pocket and pulled it out. "It asks for things to pray about here—I thought the minister would do all that."

Millie figured the church must pull in lots of prayer requests each week. It would keep the minister busy praying for all of them.

"Well, he certainly does some of it. But we all pray," Mrs. Hargrove said as she looked at the blue card. "I'm glad to see the sheriff got the cards to you. Have you filled one out yet? I'm happy to take yours and put it with the others."

"I'll do it when I finish scrubbing," Millie put the card back in her pocket. She hadn't been going to fill one out. She had told herself there was no point. She thought God didn't care about her or the things that worried her. But now she was beginning to wonder if she had been wrong. Maybe He did care.

"Can I put down a secret request?" Millie asked. She didn't know how to name some of the longings she was starting to feel. But if God were as smart as everyone seemed to think, He would know what she meant.

"Of course." Mrs. Hargrove nodded. "That sounds fine."

Millie went back to scrubbing.

"The baking soda is working," Millie said as she rinsed off the piece of floor she'd just scrubbed. Millie leaned back on her heels and stretched her back.

Mrs. Hargrove stood up and walked over to where Millie had scrubbed. "Why—my goodness—it sure is! What a blessing!"

"I'm glad it's working."

Millie liked looking around the church when it was almost empty like this. Brad had moved over by the pulpit to scrub the floor there, and Mrs. Hargrove still stood next to where Millie was scrubbing. The Christmas tree Millie had noticed on Sunday looked even more humble as it stood beside the pulpit.

"We decorated a tree last night, too," Millie told Mrs. Hargrove. "It's a homemade one like the one here. It's beautiful."

Mrs. Hargrove nodded. "Sometimes they're the best ones. The Sunday school classes made the decorations for the tree here."

"Brad made our decorations."

Brad looked up from where he was scrubbing. His knees ached, and they felt stuck to the wet floor. But even with all that, his knees went weak when he saw the look on Millie's face as she talked about the decorations. She was describing their tree to Mrs. Hargrove, and it was apparent that any annoyance she might have felt toward him this morning was not felt toward the Christmas tree back at the bunkhouse.

Millie loved that old pathetic Christmas tree.

Brad was watching Millie and didn't pay any attention to the shadow that was passing beside him.

"So, that's the way it is," Pastor Matthew said quietly.

Brad looked up. "It's the tree she likes. She doesn't have much use for me."

Pastor Matthew smiled. "Well, we don't know that for sure, do we?"

Brad figured he did know, but he didn't want to contradict the man. Brad just waited for what he was sure was coming next. A minister was supposed to say something about faith and God and how everyone should reach for the impossible. But the minister didn't say anything, so finally Brad added, "I wouldn't think there's any point in praying about something like this."

Brad waited a minute for the pastor to disagree with him. Finally, Brad could no longer contain his feeling of hope. "Is there?"

Pastor Matthew smiled. "God cares about love, if that's what you're asking."

"I wasn't thinking that—" Brad swallowed and then stopped. "I mean it wouldn't be right to ask God something like this—I mean, He doesn't cast love spells or anything, does He? Something that would make Millie stay around awhile so she could get to know me."

Pastor Matthew smiled. "Maybe not love spells, but He can work miracles, and less than that seems to be required here. After we finish, stop by my house for a few minutes, and we'll pray about it. Glory's over painting the scenery for the pageant and we can have some privacy. That is, if you want it to be private."

Brad glanced at Millie. He sure did want it to be private. He didn't know what she would think if he said a prayer about her staying in Dry Creek. Come to think of it, he didn't know what he thought about it himself. He'd never prayed about anything before that he could remember.

"God might not know me." Brad thought he should mention the fact to the minister. "We don't exactly talk."

Pastor Matthew nodded. "I figured that might be the way it is."

Brad looked around the church. It wasn't just Millie who might find it odd if he decided to pray. The guys in the bunkhouse would never understand. Brad looked back at the minister. "This is confidential, right? I mean, seeing a minister is like seeing a lawyer, isn't it? You can't tell anyone, can you?"

Pastor Matthew smiled. "My lips are sealed."

Brad nodded. That was good. He didn't need a rumor going around that Brad Parker was in such deep trouble with his love life that he had to ask God to help him. Because, of course, he wasn't in deep trouble. Not really. Was he?

Chapter Thirteen

Millie had heard about the old barn that the town of Dry Creek had turned into a community center. There hadn't been cows in the barn for years, and someone had added heaters to the building when they had the Christmas pageant inside it a couple of years ago. The wood plank floor of the barn was scrubbed clean, and the unfinished wood had a weathered look to it.

The middle of the barn was the stage, and chairs had been set up all around the walls of the barn. High, tall windows let light into the area and several bales of hay were pushed against the far wall. The faint scent of paint thinner filled the cold, moist air inside the barn.

Millie looked up and saw the pulleys on the rafters that allowed the angel to swing down over the audience during the pageant. When Forrest had tried to kill the angel, he had waited until after she made her swing out and back. In fact, the pageant was over when he'd pulled out his gun. Forrest had been able to hide behind some tall screens that had been placed around and, at first, no one had seen that he had his gun pointed at the angel.

There were no screens anymore. In fact, as Millie looked around, she saw a shiny new lock on the back door to the barn and there were no places to hide behind screens or curtains or large chairs. Even the hay was pushed firmly against the wall.

Forrest would have been saddened to see how his actions had made the people of Dry Creek feel unsafe. The lock on the barn wasn't the only new lock Millie had seen as she walked over to the barn from the church.

The day was still cold and Millie didn't have any snow boots to wear, so she had walked in the path of several tire tracks to avoid the loose snow that was lying on the ground. Brad had said he needed to discuss something with the minister and had gone off with him, telling Millie he would meet her later over at the barn.

Millie was glad to have a few minutes alone and lingered in the doorway to the barn for just a minute. The snow that was predicted for today was still not falling. The clouds had gotten grayer, though, and the air felt weighted. Something about the day matched her restlessness—like she was carrying around something cold and heavy inside of herself and she needed to let go of it just like the clouds needed to let go of their moisture.

It was those Christmas stockings, she said to herself. When she put the money in them and delivered them, she would have done all she could in memory of Forrest. She would be released from the guilt she felt on behalf of him.

When that was done, she would be able to leave Dry Creek, she told herself. The tie she felt holding her here would be gone. Her life would go back to the way it was, and she would have to try and be content.

Millie stepped all of the way inside the barn and quietly closed the door. The day was so overcast that someone had turned on the electrical lights that were attached to some of the rafters.

The pastor's wife, Glory, was kneeling in the middle of the stage area and painting what looked like a trellis. Old newspapers were spread around underneath wooden figures. Several open cans of paint sat around on the newspapers.

"May I take a look?" Millie asked.

Glory looked up from her paints and smiled.

"You can take more than a look. You're welcome to pick up a brush and join me."

Millie walked over to where Glory was painting.

Large wooden cutout figures were lying on the floor beside Glory. Some of them had been painted and some of them were still raw wood. Millie counted three sheep.

"Is that a dog?" If the cutout had been any less like a dog, Millie would have assumed it was supposed to be a sheep.

Glory nodded. "I'm afraid that over the years, our pageant has picked up some additional characters that you won't find in the Biblical account of the Nativity. One of them is a dog named Chester. He's supposed to be a sheepdog, but everyone knows Chester just shows up anywhere in the pageant."

Millie knelt down and sat the same way Glory was sitting with her legs crossed. "I thought Chester was a real dog."

Millie remembered Forrest telling her about the dog that chased the chicken in the Christmas pageant he had seen two years ago.

Glory nodded. "He is. This is the committee's way of compromising. They decided not to have any live animals in the pageant this year, but they did ask that we make a cutout of Chester just like we have a cutout of the sheep. It's to keep the children happy. They all like having Chester in the pageant."

"It seems like in a barn you would have real animals," Millie said.

Glory nodded. "It was a difficult decision to cut back this year. But people just didn't seem to have the heart to put on a full-scale pageant. Usually we invite some of the area churches, but this year we're just doing it simple and for ourselves."

Millie didn't want to ask why the people of Dry Creek were having a difficult time. She was afraid she knew.

"It's the economy," Glory added. "Everybody just seems a little more worried this year than last."

"Oh, the economy," Millie said. That wasn't so bad. "It's tough all over."

Glory looked up from her painting and smiled. "Is that what happened to you? Did you lose your job?"

Glory was friendly and her questions didn't have any sting in them.

Millie shook her head. "I still have my job. I'm on a break. It might not be much of a job, but it's waiting there for me when I go back in a few days."

"Well, that's good," Glory said as she picked

up a brush and dipped it into a small can of black paint. "It seems like around here everyone is looking for work. It's always worse at Christmas. My husband keeps thinking about adding another part-time person to the staff at the hardware store just to give someone a little help."

"That's nice of him," Millie said as she looked over the brushes. If she wasn't careful, she would be telling all of her worries to Glory, and she didn't want to do that. She would keep Forrest's secret until she could fulfill his request.

Millie nodded her head at the cutout animals. "Would you like me to paint one of the figures? If there's something simple, that is."

"Take any one of the sheep," Glory said. "Just paint it all white, and then we'll go back and paint on the hooves and the face."

Millie ran out of white paint after she painted two of the sheep.

"I think they had black sheep back then," Glory said as she passed the black can of paint. "At least it's a better color than the brown we're using for the donkey."

"There wouldn't be a black sheep at the Nativity scene, would there?" Millie asked dubiously.

Glory chuckled. "I don't know why not—the church always seems to specialize in black sheep."

Millie picked up a brush and dipped it into the

black paint. She was beginning to think that the church was nothing like she had ever thought it would be.

The afternoon light had darkened by the time Millie finished all of the sheep.

"This one looks a little hungry," Millie said. Glory had given her suggestions on how to paint the sheep's faces, but then had left it up to Millie. "I hope the children don't mind."

Each of the cutout animals had straps on the back where a child was going to hold it during the pageant.

"The twins have already suffered their own disappointment. They wanted me to make some dragons, but I drew the line. I said I'd do Chester, but that was it. No dragons." Glory gave Millie a rueful look. "I think they wanted to surprise the angel when she comes out and says 'Behold, I bring you glad tidings.'"

Millie had never actually read the Bible. "There aren't...?"

Glory shook her head. "No. But the twins swear there should have been. I think they figure if Mary and Joseph had come in riding a dragon, the innkeeper would have given them better accommodations."

"That's kind of cute."

Glory sighed and stood up. "Yeah, they're hard

to say no to. In fact—" Glory walked over to the bales and picked up two cutout figures that had been lying on top of them "—I made them these little ones for later—after the pageant."

Millie smiled at the two little dragon figures Glory had made. They were both still unpainted.

"Mrs. Hargrove is going to flunk us all in Sunday school if they use these in the pageant," Glory said.

Both Millie and Glory heard the voices of the men and looked toward the entrance of the barn. Pastor Matthew and Brad opened the door and stepped inside the barn.

"How's it coming?" Pastor Matthew asked.

"Good," Glory said.

Millie nodded and smiled.

Pastor Matthew walked over to Glory and gave her a kiss. Brad walked over to Millie, and she had a moment's panic that he meant to kiss her, as well.

"I painted a black sheep," Millie blurted out, and turned to walk back to where the animal cutouts were.

Well, Brad thought to himself, he guessed Pastor Matthew was right when he said God didn't hand out any love potions to people. Millie hadn't gazed up to him with anything near the look of adoration that Glory had on her face when she turned toward her husband.

Of course, Brad decided, it might be too soon for Millie to feel that settled, married love that Glory seemed to feel. Maybe a love potion would start out different—maybe there'd be a tingling sensation or something.

"Are you feeling okay?" Brad asked as Millie walked away from him. "Not dizzy or anything?"

"My one leg has a cramp in it," Millie said as she turned to him and then sat down. "It must be the way I was sitting. How did you know?"

"Oh, ah, there's a lot of paint fumes in here. I figured they might be affecting everyone."

"I don't think they'd give me a leg cramp," Millie said and stretched her leg out in front of her. "Unless it's some kind of slow-acting poison or something."

Brad had to congratulate himself. He'd just witnessed the opposite of a love potion. Millie wasn't even smiling at him now. In fact, she was frowning at him. He couldn't have done a worse job of it if he'd tried.

Brad sighed. He wasn't the kind of man who could be subtle. He'd just have to plough forward and hope that Pastor Matthew's God would have mercy on him.

"I wouldn't worry about it—the fumes aren't poisonous. I'm sure they haven't affected you at all. And that's good you're able to be around the paint fumes and not get sick," Brad said. He needed to get it out there before she started thinking she had the plague. "You know there's a job that's going to be opening up soon at the hardware store. Probably working with paint some. It might be a natural fit for you."

Brad decided Millie was looking at him like he'd sprouted another ear. "Some people really enjoy working in the hardware store."

"I've always worked in restaurants."

"Well, maybe Linda needs someone to help her out in the café," Brad said. She wasn't making this easy for him.

"The café's closed."

"Well, now it is, sure—but it'll open again when Linda gets back from Los Angeles."

Brad didn't know how a man could break a sweat when the air in the barn was cold. Maybe he was the one getting sick from the fumes.

"Do you think she'd hire me?" Millie asked. Brad swore he saw a flare of hope in her eyes before it died. "After all this fuss about me breaking in and all. I mean, she might think I was planning to rob her."

"Oh."

"Of course I wasn't robbing her," Millie added. "It's just that—"

Brad nodded. He needed another prayer session with the pastor. After they'd talked and prayed, Brad had begun to have hope that Millie would stay in Dry Creek long enough for the two of them to have a proper courtship. He didn't think Millie was the kind of woman who would get engaged after knowing a man for only a day or two.

No, he needed some time to show her they would be good together. It didn't seem like it was such a big miracle for God to perform. It didn't require bringing someone back to life from the dead or parting a sea or anything. All Brad needed was a little time.

"How's your car doing?" Brad asked. That car might be his best hope. If the thing broke down, Millie would be around for at least a week while they sent away for parts.

"Fine," Millie said.

Brad nodded. He'd pray about that car of hers. He wasn't even sure you could call it a miracle if the car broke down before she left Dry Creek. In fact, it would probably be a miracle if it *didn't* break down. All he needed to do was have her drive it around until it died. He might not even need any prayer to pull this off. A full tank of gas might be all he needed.

Millie decided Brad was right about the paint fumes. They certainly seemed to be affecting him.

One minute he was frowning, and the next minute he looked perfectly happy.

"I'll go open the door," Millie said as she stood up. The air outside was cold, but it was better to be a little cold than to be affected by those fumes.

When Millie opened the door, she saw that it was starting to snow. Tiny flakes were drifting to the ground. "It's snowing."

"We should get your car back to the ranch before the roads get slippery," Brad said as he walked over and stood behind her.

"I could ride back with you," Millie said.

"Really?" Brad looked happy and then he looked stern. "No, it's better if you drive your car back. Wouldn't want to leave it in Dry Creek. And your tank is almost full, isn't it?"

Millie nodded. She knew to fill her tank in Miles City. Brad was right. She did like to have her car close by just in case. Besides, she still had those stockings in the trunk.

"You might want to drive it out to the barn when you get back to the ranch, too. Get some more practice driving in the snow. And then you'll want to drive it back tonight for the pageant."

Millie nodded again. She definitely needed her car tonight. It was nice of Brad to realize that, especially since he'd seemed so intent this morning on keeping her car off of the roads.

Chapter Fourteen

Millie stood outside the bunkhouse of the Elkton Ranch and stared down at the contents of her car's trunk. The sun was setting and light snow was still falling. It had been snowing for several hours, but Charlie had said the roads were not in danger of being blocked.

Charlie seemed particularly pleased that there was no reason to worry about the roads. He'd already convinced all of the men in the bunkhouse to drive into Dry Creek tonight to see the Christmas pageant.

It was the Christmas pageant that was causing Millie's frown. She had just slipped a hundred-dollar bill into each of the red stockings she'd made, and she'd stacked the stockings alphabetically in two neat piles in the trunk of her car. She was all ready to deliver the stockings, but she didn't know how to do it now.

At first, she had thought she would go to the barn before the pageant and lay the stockings around the room on the chairs. But then she realized it would create a lot of fuss, and she didn't want to take anything away from the pageant.

No, she decided, she'd have to deliver the stockings after the pageant. Maybe she could just leave them inside the barn door on the bench where people sat when they needed to take off their snow boots. Everyone would see them on their way out of the barn.

When Millie made her decision, she expected the heavy feeling inside of her to lift. She had almost completed her task. It hadn't gone as Forrest probably thought it would, but she would be able to deliver the hundred-dollar bills and finish what she had started. She should feel good, not sad.

After all, things were working out. Millie figured she was still a stranger to most people in Dry Creek—at least as much of a stranger as Forrest had been when he had been here. He'd only been in the little town a few days, as well. When she left, even the people she had met would eventually forget her name and what she looked like.

She would truly be a Christmas stranger.

And that, Millie finally admitted, was why she was sad. The people of Dry Creek might forget her, but she would never forget them. Not Glory, or Charlie, or Mrs. Hargrove. And especially not Brad.

Of course, Brad would forget her, Millie decided in a burst of irritation. The man couldn't wait for her to get in her car and drive off somewhere. He didn't even seem to care where she was going. She could have suggested she drive to the moon, and he would have encouraged her to do it. Just to please him, she'd already driven up and down the driveway into the Elkton ranch several times this afternoon.

Millie looked over toward the bunkhouse. The last time she'd parked her car this afternoon, she'd deliberately parked so she could see in the big window in the living room. Frost had edged the window, but she could still see the little Christmas tree on the opposite wall.

That tree would always be her favorite Christmas tree, even though Millie vowed she would decorate one for herself next Christmas. Something about this Christmas had changed the feeling she had inside that she needed to be on the outside looking in at Christmas.

Maybe it was going to church here and seeing

the people all work together. Or being Christmas company at the bunkhouse. Or even riding out to get the Christmas tree with Brad.

Maybe it was all of it. She supposed it didn't matter. What mattered was that she no longer felt so alone. Not even, she swallowed, when she was leaving.

There, she thought to herself, she'd said it. She was leaving Dry Creek.

She really had no choice. She knew the job at the hardware store was a charity job and was meant for someone in Dry Creek. The pastor hadn't created the job to give it to someone who had just come into town. It might be an option to work at the café, but Linda was gone and there was no one to ask about working there.

It wasn't the stockings in the trunk that were bothering her, Millie finally admitted. It was her small suitcase that was sitting next to them. Millie had slipped the suitcase out of the bunkhouse earlier this afternoon without anyone seeing her.

She needed to be ready to leave Dry Creek. The longer she stayed, the harder it would be to leave.

Millie wondered if Forrest was looking down from heaven and seeing what a mess she'd made of her version of the plan. She knew now that Forrest had wanted her to meet the people of Dry Creek.

She had wanted to sneak into town and leave before anyone saw her. She would have succeeded, too, if Brad hadn't been parked behind the café.

For the first time it struck her just how odd that was. What had Brad been doing parked there? He couldn't have been having trouble with his pickup, because the old thing had started right up when he turned the ignition. And, if he'd had a flat tire, he wouldn't have been parked behind the café. Brad must have been sitting there for a long time, because she knew he hadn't driven back there while she was inside.

There was only one reason Millie could think of for Brad to be there, and she didn't like it.

Millie slammed the trunk of her car and headed back to the bunkhouse.

The main room of the bunkhouse was empty, but Millie heard someone in the kitchen.

Charlie stood at the stove stirring a big pot of something. Whatever it was, it smelled good, but Millie hardly noticed.

"I have a question for you," Millie said. She couldn't think of a subtle way to ask what she needed to know. "Around here, when you see a car that's pulled off the road at night, what do you think?"

Charlie looked up from his stirring. "Car trouble."

Millie shook her head. "There was no car trouble."

"Maybe it's late and no one's in the car," Charlie suggested.

Millie shook her head again. "Oh, someone was in the car all right."

Charlie smiled. "Well, if there's two someones in the car, then you have your answer. There's nothing quite as romantic as sitting together under the stars."

Millie nodded her head. She didn't know what had happened to the woman that had been in the pickup with Brad. "Do people around here ever drive into Dry Creek and leave their cars at the café before they go into Miles City?"

"Sure, if they're going to drive together most of the way." Charlie looked at her quizzically. "You worried about your car dying or something? If you are, anyone would be happy to give you a lift anywhere you need to go."

Millie shook her head. "No, my car is fine. Thanks."

Charlie shrugged. "Well, if you need anything, let me know."

Millie nodded. What she needed wasn't something Charlie could give her.

Millie walked back into the main room of the bunkhouse and sat down on a sofa. What she needed was to leave Dry Creek and Brad Parker before the cracks that were starting in her heart caused it to break in two.

Brad stopped and scraped his feet before he entered the bunkhouse. He'd been forced to drive back from Miles City all by himself. You'd think the other guys had never smelled women's perfume before. Brad had been determined to find the perfume that suited Millie best, and how was he supposed to tell what each one smelled like if he didn't have the sales clerk spray the air in front of him?

The other guys had gone together and bought Millie a wool scarf and some mittens, but Brad wanted a special gift, and that was a challenge in the small department store in Miles City.

Finally, Brad had settled on something called "Snow Angel" that the salesclerk swore was light and sounded, from everything he had told her, like it would be perfect for Millie.

Brad saw that Millie had been looking at the Christmas tree before he came in. When she heard him, she turned around.

"Sorry to let the cold air in," Brad said. When he had opened the door to the bunkhouse, a gust of wind had followed him in. "The wind's blowing out there."

"You must be cold," Millie said as she stood up. "I could start the coffeepot."

Brad shook his head. "I'll just warm up by the fire."

Brad had the bottle of perfume in his pocket. The clerk had wrapped the perfume for him, but he decided to wait until after the pageant to put the box under the tree. He didn't want Millie to think she needed to give him a present, so he didn't want her to know about the box.

Millie sniffed the air. The closer she walked to Brad, the more she could smell the perfume. It wasn't some kind of cologne for a man, either. No, the perfume was definitely the kind a woman would wear.

"I thought you were out with the other guys," Millie said.

"Oh, I was," Brad said. Millie thought he looked a little guilty, but he continued, "We had some business to take care of."

Millie wondered what the woman's name was. Not that it was any of her business, she reminded herself. "Well, that's good then, I guess."

Just then the rest of the ranch hands came into

the bunkhouse. Millie noticed as each one filed through the door that none of them smelled of perfume. Which meant that, wherever Brad had been, he hadn't been with them.

Millie decided, as she blinked a few times, that it was just as well that she was leaving tonight after the pageant.

Chapter Fifteen

The pageant was scheduled to begin at seven o'clock, and by then the sky was completely dark. The snow flurries had stopped an hour earlier, and the clouds had parted enough to allow a few stars to shine through the blackness. The lights inside the barn showed through the high windows, and Millie could see into the barn each time someone opened the main door.

Millie parked her car as close to the barn as she could. She was surprised that Brad had offered to give her a ride to the pageant. She almost asked him why he wasn't giving a ride to Miss Perfume. But she didn't. She couldn't ride with him anyway, because she had the Christmas stockings. The Christmas stockings were supposed to be a surprise, and she no longer felt any desire to tell Brad all her secrets.

Brad would know soon enough anyway. Millie had decided the town of Dry Creek should know that Forrest was sorry, and so she'd enclosed a note in Mrs. Hargrove's stocking explaining everything.

The air was chilly when Millie opened the door to her car, and she walked quickly to the barn. She'd come back later and get the stockings.

The light inside the barn was dim, and Millie could see the trellis in the middle of the floor that had a sign hanging from it saying Bethlehem Inn. From the sounds of the shuffling feet and giggles coming from behind a makeshift curtain at the end of the barn, the animals were getting ready to play their parts.

A stereo was set up in the barn and Millie could hear the muted sounds of Christmas carols. She also heard the sound of Brad's voice and saw him talking with a group of men gathered near a coffeepot in one corner of the barn. There was no one standing near him who might be Miss Perfume, but then, Millie reasoned, the woman might be one of the ones she saw helping the children get into their costumes.

Millie walked over to a place where there were several empty chairs. Walking through the people of Dry Creek wasn't as easy as it sounded. People smiled at her and greeted her every step of the way. She'd refused several offers of a chair by the time she reached the one she wanted.

Millie picked a chair that had empty chairs on both sides of it. She didn't want to get to know any more people in Dry Creek. She'd just be leaving soon anyway.

Someone turned the music up louder and flicked the light switches. That must be the signal that the pageant was ready to begin. The people who weren't already seated started to move to the sides of the barn where the chairs were positioned.

"May I?"

Millie heard Brad's low question as he sat down in the chair next to her.

Brad didn't know why Millie had such a surprised look on her face. He'd followed her car into Dry Creek to be sure she didn't have any mechanical trouble on the way. He'd even sat in his pickup for a little bit after they both parked until it became clear that she was not going to go inside right away. The only reason he'd gone in ahead of her was because he was beginning to feel like a stalker.

She should have figured out by now that he was planning to sit beside her.

"You're wearing perfume." Brad noticed the

fact as everyone around them was sitting down. He hadn't thought she had been wearing perfume before. The scent she was wearing now was light and fruity. Maybe she wouldn't like the perfume he had bought for her. He should have asked if she had a preference. "What kind is it?"

"It's not perfume. It's peach soap."

"Ah, soap." Brad didn't know if that meant she would like perfume or not. Well, it was too late now anyway. He planned to give her the perfume tonight when they got back to the bunkhouse. He could only hope for the best.

The lights were dimmed almost completely for a minute.

Brad assumed by the sounds that the children were getting in place for the pageant.

The donkey was the first thing to come out from behind the curtain. The donkey was followed by nine-year-old Angie Loden wearing a blue tablecloth wrapped sari-style around her. A pillow made her look awkwardly pregnant, but the look in her eye made her look like a schoolteacher.

Millie smiled when she saw the little girl in blue. She wondered if girls playing at being Mary always wore blue because they had all seen the same stained glass picture of Jesus talking to the little girl in the blue robe.

Millie heard the choked-back laughter as the

girl started her walk. She obviously wasn't as
worried about talking to Jesus as she was about
correcting the boy who was playing Joseph. Millie could almost hear the girl scolding him in a low
whisper as the boy tried to keep up with the girl
and the donkey. The boy was having a hard time
not tripping on the hem of his robe, until finally
Mary reached over and adjusted the belt around
the robe so that material bunched up around the
boy's waist, making the robe shorter.

One of the Curtis twins was carrying the cutout
figure of the donkey, and he was leading the girl
along the path toward the makeshift inn.

The Christmas music was turned almost completely off, and another voice came from the loud-
speakers. Millie decided the voice was from a
tape, because she didn't recognize it from the
voices she'd heard in Dry Creek.

"At that time, Augustus Caesar sent an order
that all people in the countries under Roman rule
must list their names in the register," the voice
said, as Mary, Joseph and the donkey slowly
walked toward the inn.

Millie had not realized the whole Nativity
scene started because someone wanted to collect
everyone's name. She thought of the stockings in
her trunk. They made a more appropriate Christmas gift than she had thought. She'd had to col-

lect all the names of the people, as well. She knew how much trouble that could be. It gave her a certain empathy with Augustus Caesar.

Millie sat back and decided to enjoy the pageant. She chuckled along with everyone else when the innkeeper looked uncertain about whether or not he had any rooms. Finally, Mary looked down some imaginary hall and said she could see his inn was filled with tourists, and so there were no rooms for those people who really needed a place to stay.

The angel didn't fly overhead like she had in other pageants, but a blond girl climbed a ladder and flapped her wings while shouting out "Behold!" with as much enthusiasm as the original angel must have had.

Chester, the real dog, chose this moment to run inside and shake the snow off of his coat.

Millie expected the adults to scold and ask who had let Chester into the barn, but they all just seemed to shrug their shoulders and turn their attention back to the unfolding pageant.

It must have been when the shepherds were coming in from their fields that Brad put his arm on the back of her chair. Millie could feel it on her shoulders. She'd been laughing at Chester's efforts to herd the wooden sheep, and she looked up at Brad.

Brad was happy. He'd moved his arm from the back of Millie's chair to her shoulders and she'd smiled up at him. Her face was still glowing from the laughter, and even though he wasn't the reason for her laughter, the delight she was feeling spilled over onto him.

Brad began to wonder if he was wrong about how long it took for a man to fall in love. He'd thought he needed to get to know Millie. But he was beginning to think he knew all he needed to know right now.

If the sheep hadn't arrived at the inn just then, Brad would have whispered something silly in Millie's ear. But she'd turned her gaze back to the pageant, and he wanted her to remember every single moment of this night. He'd wait and whisper in her ear tonight after he'd given her the perfume.

Millie sighed when the wise men started walking toward the inn. The littlest of the boys had trouble keeping his crown on his head and had to set his golden box of spices down on the floor so he could adjust his crown. Chester, of course, had to come over and sniff at the spices until he sneezed. Whatever it was that was supposed to be myrrh scattered across the floor.

All in all, Millie thought when the lights were dimmed for the last time, the pageant had been delightful. It had also gone much too fast.

Millie looked over at Brad. She'd have to say goodbye to him later. Maybe she wouldn't have to leave right after she delivered the stockings. But, for now, she should make her move while the children all came back on stage to sing "Silent Night."

The air outside the barn felt sharply cold to Millie after she had been inside. Brad had thought she was leaving to use the restroom, or he would have come with her. Setting the stockings out for everyone was something she had to do by herself. Forrest had been her friend, and she would help him do what he could to make his actions up to the people of Dry Creek. She had left Mrs. Hargrove's stocking on top of all the others, since it had the note inside it.

Millie could barely hold all of the stockings in her arms, but she didn't want to make two trips. She planned to leave them on the bench inside the door. Now that the pageant was almost over, it wouldn't be long before someone turned and saw the stockings.

Millie had left the door slightly open so that she could just push it completely open with her arms. She managed to come back inside the barn and stand by the door without anyone noticing her.

Everyone inside the barn was looking at the

children singing in the middle of the floor, and Millie could see why. With their crooked angel wings and dragging shepherd robes, the children were charming. Even Chester was sitting calmly beside the wooden sheep while they sang.

Millie set the stack of stockings down on the bench. There were mittens and scarves on the shelf above the bench and some rubber boots under the bench. But the bench itself was clear until Millie set down her stockings.

When children finished their last notes of "Silent Night," Millie stepped back outside the door. She left the door cracked open so she could hear people's excitement. Within minutes, she heard the first exclamation.

"Look at these!" a woman's voice said.

"Don't touch them," a man's voice answered.

"Why, they're Millie's stockings," Mrs. Hargrove said.

Millie smiled. The older woman would convince everyone to trust that the stockings were okay.

"Look what's inside them!" That voice sounded like it came from a teenage boy. "It's hundred-dollar bills!"

"What's money like that doing here?" the man who had spoken earlier said.

"I wonder if the stores are still open. I'd love

to get the kids real presents for Christmas and not just new mittens," a woman said.

"Maybe I'll get my train set," a little voice said.

Millie heard a chorus of excited whispers until the man spoke again

"But what's the money doing here?" the man insisted loudly. "If we don't know what it's doing here, we shouldn't touch it."

"It's from Millie," Mrs. Hargrove said. "She left a note."

Millie could hear the people crowding next to Mrs. Hargrove.

"Is it counterfeit?" someone asked.

"No," Mrs. Hargrove said slowly. "It's money from Forrest."

"Who's Forrest?" someone else asked.

"That's the name of the hit man," someone else answered. "But what's that got to do with that woman?"

"Millie was his friend," Mrs. Hargrove said. "And she writes that Forrest wanted us to know he was sorry for what he did here."

There was almost total silence on the other side of the door.

Finally, Brad spoke. His voice was low, but Millie could hear it clearly.

"She was friends with a hit man?" Brad's voice contained a world of confusion and disbelief. "What kind of person is friends with a hit man?"

Millie turned to walk down the stairs. She'd heard enough. It was time to leave.

The air was just as cold when Millie walked back to her car, but she didn't notice a thing. The cold outside didn't begin to compare with the cold inside of her.

She opened the door to her car and was grateful that the car started right up when she turned the ignition. She backed the car away from the barn before she turned on the headlights. She didn't want her car lights to shine into the windows of the barn. She would leave Dry Creek as quietly as she had come.

Millie rolled down the window as she pulled away from the barn. She wanted to hear any last music that might be coming from the pageant. She thought they would turn the stereo on again with the Christmas carols, but she didn't hear anything.

Finally, she rolled her window back up. She'd have to listen to her radio instead.

Chapter Sixteen

Brad sat down on the steps outside the church. He wasn't planning to go to church this morning, but it had snowed last night, and he figured he'd shovel off the steps just to show God and Mrs. Hargrove that he didn't hold any hard feelings toward them. Well, not many hard feelings anyway. Which wasn't bad considering he had met the woman of his dreams and neither one of them had helped him to keep track of her.

Millie had slipped away from the barn on Christmas Eve, and Brad hadn't even known it for a full fifteen minutes. She'd said she was going to the restroom, and he'd believed her. By the time he realized she wasn't inside the barn, he'd gone racing outside only to see that her car was gone.

He'd gotten into his pickup and followed the road all of the way into Miles City thinking he would find her. When he didn't see her, he figured she had gone the other direction out of Dry Creek, and he came barreling back and drove all the way into North Dakota before he turned around.

That old car of hers went faster than he'd thought possible.

Brad stopped shoveling and leaned on his shovel. The days had been gloomy ever since Christmas. He'd always dreaded Christmas. But now he knew it wasn't Christmas that was his problem. It was all of the rest of the days that stretched out after Christmas was gone that were going to give him grief.

Even with all of the excitement in Dry Creek these days, Brad was miserable. Every time someone talked about what they had spent their hundred dollars on, Brad thought of Millie. He'd thought of her through conversations about toy dolls and new tennis shoes. Mrs. Hargrove even informed him about the new ice-crushing blender she'd bought with part of her money.

Brad still had his hundred-dollar bill in his shirt pocket next to his heart.

Brad had wished a million times since that night that he hadn't been shocked Millie had been friends with a hit man. He shouldn't have even been surprised. He knew Millie would be loyal to her friends, and that she took up with the under-dogs. It only made sense that she would stand by her friends if they were arrested.

He wished he could tell her, though, that it was her note that made the difference to the people of Dry Creek, and not the money. Just hearing that the hit man had been deeply sorry allowed people to start trusting in strangers again.

Brad started moving his shovel again. The thing he really regretted, however, was that he'd never asked Millie for her address. He was sitting here with his heart full of things to tell her, and he didn't even know how to find her. All he really knew was that she lived somewhere around the waterfront in Seattle.

Brad had finished shoveling all of the steps when he saw the pastor come out of the parsonage and start walking toward the church.

"Good morning," Pastor Matthew called out. "You're joining us this morning for church, aren't you?"

Brad grimaced as the minister came closer. "I'm not fit for polite company these days."

Brad ran his hand over his face. He hadn't shaved for a couple of days, and he figured he looked pretty rough.

"Having a hard time?" the pastor asked as he came closer to Brad.

Brad nodded. "Not much I can do about it though."

The pastor looked at Brad for a minute. "If you want to come to my office with me, I think I have something that might cheer you up."

"No offense," Brad said as he leaned against his shovel, "but this is something prayer can't fix."

"God might surprise you," the pastor said as he started climbing the steps.

Brad figured God had already had His chance to work on Millie and had missed His opportunity completely.

"What you might not understand is that I need concrete help," Brad said as he started to follow the pastor. "I mean prayer is nice, but I need, well, real help."

The pastor had walked up the steps to the church and opened the main door. Brad still followed him as the minister crossed the back of the church and opened a door into a small room.

Pastor Matthew went to his desk, picked something up and turned around to face Brad.

"Is this concrete enough for you?" the pastor held out a blue card.

"Millie filled out a visitor's form?"

The tightness Brad had felt in his chest all week started to loosen.

The pastor nodded. "Of course, it wouldn't be

right for me to give the information on this card to just anyone."

"Oh."

"However, I figure that a representative from the church should be allowed to call on Millie, since she did mark the box that asked for a visit from someone from the church."

"I've been to the church twice now—if the Christmas pageant counts."

Pastor Matthew grinned as he held the card out to Brad. "All you really need to do is invite Millie to next Sunday's service. I can even send a church bulletin along with you, so you have all the information."

Brad understood why people throughout the ages had kissed the feet of holy men when they got their prayers answered. "Thank you."

Ruby's café was on the Seattle waterfront, and most mornings in January the air was cold. The floor at Ruby's was made of thick wooden planks and the walls were filled with large paned glass windows. Ruby believed in natural light, plants and strong coffee. It was the coffee that brought the customers in, but Millie suspected it was the plants that made them want to linger over their meals.

Not that Millie was worried about customers who wouldn't leave.

She had just mixed up the order on table seven. Instead of bringing the man coffee with cream, she had brought him tea with sugar. In all of her years at Ruby's she'd never made a mistake on an order until after she got back from Dry Creek. Since she'd gotten back eight days ago, however, she'd made thirty-two mistakes. The reason she knew the exact number was because the other waitresses were trying to guess the limit of Ruby's patience and they were counting.

Of course, the waitresses all knew Millie's job was safe because they were running shorthanded. The dishwasher had quit, and Ruby had no sooner put the Help Wanted—Dishwasher sign in the window than one of the waitresses had quit, as well.

Not that the other waitresses weren't also sympathetic. They'd cooed and fussed over Millie that first day back until she thought she would have to take to her bed and have herself a good rest just to get some peace from people's good intentions.

Millie had distracted the other waitresses from their sympathy by telling them about the Christmas pageant at Dry Creek. When she left Montana, she fully intended to entertain them all with stories about Brad. But she found the stories she had thought were so funny when they happened now only made her feel sad. Even the story about the spiders would have made her cry if she tried to tell it.

Millie had slipped once when she was talking to Louise and had mentioned that she'd stayed in the bunkhouse in the room of a nice man.

The waitresses at Ruby's weren't usually impressed with someone who was just nice, but they seemed to know there was more to Millie's stories than she was telling.

The door to Ruby's buzzed whenever anyone opened it and came inside. Ruby said the buzzer allowed them to have good customer control. No customer was ever supposed to wait more than five minutes at Ruby's before he or she was seated and offered a cup of coffee.

So it was only natural that all of the waitresses looked up when the buzzer sounded.

Millie's mouth dropped open. In all of the days since she'd left Dry Creek, she never thought she'd look up at Ruby's and see Brad Parker walk into the café.

"What are you doing here?" Millie walked over to the man and asked.

For the hundredth time that day, Brad wondered if his plan was a good one. It was a long drive from Dry Creek to Seattle, and he'd thought of a million clever things to say to Millie when he saw her. But then he'd decided to just be himself and be honest. When he saw how white Millie's face was, however, he wished he had thought of something to tell her that didn't contain the words "I came because of you."

"I came for the job," Brad blurted out. He'd seen the sign in the window of the diner, and he was only beginning to see the advantages it offered.

"What job?" Millie frowned.

"Dishwasher," Brad guessed. He was almost sure that was what the sign said.

That seemed to leave Millie speechless. Finally, she swallowed. "Here?"

Brad nodded. "I think that's where the job is."

Millie just stared at him.

"I'm hoping they'll take me temporarily. For a few weeks," Brad added. "I could use a break from moving cattle."

Millie might be speechless, but Brad could hear the other waitresses start to chatter. Finally, one of them walked over to him.

Brad saw by the woman's badge that her name was Sherry. Ordinarily, she would be the kind of woman who would catch his eye. Her hair was all highlights and curls. Her fingernails were deep red and slightly pointed. Her smile was friendly and her uniform not buttoned up tight.

"I'm sure Ruby will hire you on the spot," the waitress said as she stepped closer to Brad. "I sure would."

"Back off, Sherry," an older waitress said. "This is a *nice* man."

Brad thought she said the word "nice" like it was a code.

"A *nice* man from Dry Creek, I believe," the older woman said as she gave Sherry a stern look.

Sherry shrugged her shoulders and turned away. "Can't blame a girl for trying."

Millie decided she better set down the coffee-pot that she was holding. Come to think of it, she should just sit her whole self down.

Louise seemed to agree. She looked at Millie and said, "Now's a good time to take your break. We're not busy. There's no one on the patio."

Millie nodded as she turned toward the patio.

"Take your time. I'll send out some of those fresh donuts for you and your friend."

Millie walked out to the patio, and even though she heard his footsteps behind her, she was still surprised to see Brad himself behind her there when she came to the table and sat down.

"Mind if I join you?" Brad said.

Millie blinked. She hadn't noticed how nervous he seemed. She had always thought she was the only one who got nervous. "Please do."

Brad sat down at the small table across from Millie.

"What brings you to Seattle?" Millie finally asked.

"You."

Brad knew he'd been clumsy. He hadn't meant to rush Millie like that. "I mean, I came to see you because you asked for a visit from someone from the church."

Brad pulled out the blue visitor's card that Millie had filled out when she was in Dry Creek. The corners were bent because he'd kept it on the dash of his pickup all the way from Montana to Seattle.

"You came to invite me back to church?" Millie sounded incredulous.

"I came to invite you back to Dry Creek," Brad said quietly.

Millie didn't answer right away so he just kept on explaining. "I know it's too big of a decision to make right away. I know you've only known me for a couple of days. But you aren't going to get to know me better unless you're in Dry Creek or I'm here." Brad took a deep breath. "So I thought

I'd stay here for a while so we can get to know each other."

Millie started to smile. She felt like someone had turned the sunshine on in the middle of an overcast day. "We're going to get to know each other?"

Brad nodded and started to smile himself.

"You're willing to wash dishes so you can get to know me better?" Millie still couldn't believe it. Most men she knew wouldn't wash dishes for any reason. "You know Ruby throws in the pots and pans, too. It's not just the easy stuff like glasses and silverware."

"I'd figured as much," Brad said as his smile turned into a full grin.

"You do get a share of the tips though," Millie added. "And meals—you get meals."

"I'd settle for a kiss or two from the right waitress," Brad said, and then he remembered something and reached in his pocket. "And I have a Christmas present for you."

Millie looked at the silver box with the red ribbon on it. No one had ever given her such a pretty gift.

Brad handed her the box.

"Go ahead, open it," Brad said.

Millie had half of the paper off when she

started to smell the perfume. She recognized it from the fragrance that had surrounded Brad on the night of the Christmas pageant. *She* was the perfume woman in Brad's life! She had to blink a little to keep the tears away.

"You're not allergic, are you?" Brad asked.

Millie shook her head. She only had one problem at the moment. "I don't have a present for you."

Millie figured the hundred-dollar bill didn't count because that was really from Forrest. She hadn't expected to meet Brad when she went to Dry Creek, so she hadn't taken a present with her. And she hadn't expected to ever see him again when she left, so there was no reason to buy him one later.

There was only one gift she could think of that might please him, and she couldn't think about it too long or she'd decide it wasn't grand enough.

Millie stood up and leaned across the table. Then she bent down and kissed Brad square on the lips.

Millie had to swallow a chuckle, because she knew she had startled Brad for a second. But the man adapted quick. Before she knew it, the kiss was making her head spin and her knees buckle.

"Oh, my," Millie said when the kiss had ended.

She was leaning into Brad and she was halfway into his arms. He moved around the table and settled her on his lap.

"You know, I have a feeling I'm not going to mind washing all those dishes at all," Brad said.

Millie just smiled. She had a feeling she wouldn't mind him washing all those dishes, either.

Epilogue

Four Months Later

Millie smiled as she looked at her bridal dress in the mirror. She had been staying at Mrs. Hargrove's for the past two weeks while she and Brad received marriage counseling from Pastor Matthew and made final plans for their wedding.

She and Brad had been going to a church in Seattle, but they both wanted to be married in the church in Dry Creek, especially after Millie started receiving the notes of thanks from the people in town. She was pleased that the notes were as likely to thank her for letting them know that the hit man was sorry as they were to thank her for the money.

The people in Dry Creek were good, solid people.

Millie and Brad intended to live their lives in Dry Creek and wanted to make the church their home. Since neither one of them had ideal childhoods, they knew that church would be their family.

Millie marveled at how much her understanding of God could change in just a few months. She and Brad had both asked God to help them understand more about Him, and they'd been astonished at what they were learning.

Millie fingered the lace on her veil. She had never thought she would know a man who wanted to take care of her as much as she wanted to take care of him. Brad had put a down payment on a ranch just outside of Dry Creek, and that would be where they would raise their family.

"Are you ready?" Mrs. Hargrove called up the stairs. "The carriage is here to pick you up."

When the ranch hands had heard that she and Brad were going to get married, they had rigged up one of the ranch wagons as a wedding carriage. Millie had seen the wagon this morning. It was covered with cascades of spring flowers. Pinks. Lavenders. And blues.

Millie refused to ride in the wagon without Brad, even for the short distance to the church, so everyone had decided to forget all the usual traditions, and she and Brad were riding to the church together. After the reception, they'd ride to their new home in the wagon, as well.

It would be a good start for them, Millie thought as she gave her face a final glance in the mirror and then headed down the stairs to her own true love.

* * * * *

Dear Reader,

Do you ever feel that God is asking you to do something that is just too difficult? I do. Like Millie in the book, I sometimes feel like I am a humble waitress and am being asked to do something that God should know requires being a king—or at least an elder statesman. The peculiar thing about God, however, is that He does mix it up. He uses the most unlikely people to do what He wants done.

Of course, while this is sometimes alarming and often frustrating, it is also what makes life with God unique. He isn't impressed with your credentials or stature; He is impressed with your heart. If you are willing, He will lead you—and heap blessings upon you in the process.

Sincerely,

Janet Tronstad